"*P sst!*" Craig stood in the
two classrooms.

"Flack! Come here!" It ca
per, one you could hear half

Jerry frowned. "Why? I l
room."

"Come on!"

Jerry sighed and walked
room behind him was dark
Jerry saw that no one was

Except Gabe.

The boys rushed at
hauled him into the room

"What do you want?"
free his arms.

Gabe was very stron
him, he didn't have an
across the room and ove

That's when Jerry re
open.

OTHER NOVELS BY CAROL GORMAN

DORK
ON THE RUN

Carol Gorman

HarperTrophy®
An Imprint of HarperCollinsPublishers

J
Gorman

To the brilliant Susan Rich,
who endeared herself to me the first time she signed her e-mail
"Your dorky editor . . ."

Harper Trophy® is a registered trademark of HarperCollins Publishers Inc.

Dork on the Run
Copyright © 2002 by Carol Gorman

Library of Congress Cataloging-in-Publication Data
Gorman, Carol.
    Dork on the run / Carol Gorman.
        p.   cm.
    Summary: Having reluctantly agreed to run for sixth-grade president, Jerry,
who has been trying to change his image as a dork, finds his opponent playing
dirty tricks on him.
    ISBN 0-06-029409-4 — ISBN 0-06-029410-8 (lib. bdg.) — ISBN 0-06-440970-8 (pbk.)
    [1. Elections—Fiction.   2. Politics, Practical—Fiction.   3. Schools—Fiction.
4. Popularity—Fiction.   5. Practical jokes—Fiction.]   I. Title.
PZ7.G6693 Dq   2002   2001051456

Typography by Hilary Zarycky
❖
First Harper Trophy edition, 2003

Visit us on the World Wide Web!
www.harperchildrens.com

ACKNOWLEDGMENTS

Many thanks to Terry Kemme and Bonnie Dodge for their help. I'd also like to thank Gary Rieck, chemistry teacher at Washington High School, and Associate Professor Maria A. Dean at Coe College for some of the science content and demonstrations of several cool experiments.

Chapter One

Jerry Flack stood before his locker, perplexed. He had come to this very spot three times a day for the past four weeks, worked the combination, and unlocked his locker. He had successfully opened it dozens of times since he'd started Hawthorne Middle School. It had never been a problem.

So why couldn't he remember his locker combination today?

The hallway was crowded with students. They charged past in a noisy blur as they made their way down the hall to their lockers and first-period classes.

"Hey, Jer." Jerry didn't have to look up to know

who had suddenly appeared at his side. Only one person in school called him Jer. That was Craig Fox, his locker partner. Craig had started calling him that last week, just before asking Jerry if he could borrow $1.50 for lunch. He hadn't paid Jerry back yet.

"Hey, Craig." Jerry continued to stare at the combination lock. It looked fuzzy around the edges. *What was the combination?* He didn't want to admit to Craig that he couldn't remember. He'd never hear the end of it.

Craig grabbed Jerry's glasses off his face and held them high over his head. "How about five bucks to get your glasses back? Want 'em? Hunh?"

He tossed the glasses over Jerry's head. A long arm reached out of the crowd of students and snatched them from midair.

Jerry turned, and through a gauzy, myopic haze, he saw Gabe Marshall grinning at him. Gabe wiggled the glasses in front of Jerry's face.

"Come on, Gabe," Jerry said. "I can't see without my glasses."

"I'd say they're worth more than five bucks then," Gabe said. He tossed the glasses back to Craig.

"Yeah," Craig said. "Ten bucks to get 'em back."

He hurled them high over Jerry's head again. This time, they sailed past Gabe and clattered onto the scuffed tile floor. Jerry knew in an instant, as he watched a crowd of students moving shoulder-to-shoulder, their two-dozen feet tromping like an advancing army, that his glasses were goners.

Even over the pandemonium of talk and laughter and slamming lockers, he heard the crunch of his glasses under their feet. After the throng passed, Jerry made his way to the scattered pieces that littered the floor.

He bent and picked up one section of the broken frames. The lenses had been kicked out of his range of blurry vision.

Could this day be any worse? It was more horrible than the bad old days at his former school where he'd been branded a dork and left to travel with the other geeks and nerds, sometimes laughed at, sometimes ignored.

The intercom popped on nearby. "We're in for a great day, weatherwise," a voice said. "Sunny, with highs in the upper sixties."

Jerry's eyes snapped open, and he gazed around his bedroom. Fuzzy sunshine peeked around his shade in a long, narrow strip at the window's edge. The blurry faces of Albert Einstein and Stephen Hawking gazed down from posters on the wall over his desk, and his computer's screen saver displayed a dozen hazy green lizards, scurrying in every direction.

"And now for the traffic report," came the announcer's cheerful voice from the clock radio on the nightstand near Jerry's left ear.

Jerry let out a stream of breath and turned on his side, a colossal wave of relief sweeping over him.

It had only been a terrible dream.

He wasn't a dork now. He had overcome Dorkiness at his new school, and he had lots of good friends. His locker combination was right 66, left 32, right 5. Everything was cool.

He waited for his nerves to calm, for the adrenaline to stop rushing through his body, for his breathing to return to normal. He was exhausted.

But that was okay. He would go to school, have a great day, and remind himself that things were different than they used to be. Spencer Lake was his new home, and the sixth-grade class at Hawthorne Middle School had lots of kids who liked him. Life was good.

Jerry smiled to himself, climbed out of bed, and put on his glasses. Instantly, the room snapped into sharp focus. He dressed in a pair of distressed jeans and a T-shirt that said, "Yada, yada, yada," and loped down the stairs to the kitchen.

His mom was setting up the coffeemaker. Six-year-old Melissa stood at the kitchen table, pouring cornflakes into a bowl.

"Morning," his mother said to him. "Before Dad left, he said he wants to finish building the tree house tonight."

"Yay!" Melissa hollered. "Tonight the tree house

will be *mine*. My very own room. I can't wait."

Jerry selected Cheerios from the cupboard and shook the cereal into a bowl. "Melissa," he said, "you already have your very own room."

"Not in a *tree*."

"Can you come home right after school and help?" his mom asked.

"Yeah," Jerry said. He reached into the refrigerator and pulled out a carton of milk.

"Mom, after the tree house is finished, can I eat breakfast up there?" Melissa asked.

"We'll see."

Melissa frowned and turned to her brother. "Jerry, you've been around Mom longer than I have. When she says, 'We'll see,' does that usually mean yes or no?"

"I don't have the empirical data to draw a conclusion on that," Jerry said. He finished pouring the milk on his cereal and sat at the kitchen table. "But off the top of my head, I'd say she won't let you eat breakfast in the tree."

"That's not fair." Melissa turned to her mother. "I think—"

"I didn't say no," her mother said. "At least, not yet."

Melissa looked at Jerry. "She'll say no, won't she?"

"Yup," Jerry said, plunging his spoon into the cereal. "Most likely."

Melissa rolled her eyes and blew out an exasperated breath that lifted her bangs off her forehead for a moment. "I need a lawyer," she said. "First graders have rights, too."

"That's what you think," Jerry said.

After breakfast, Jerry walked to school as usual. Residue from his dream still clung a bit to his brain, and he concentrated hard to shake it off.

Everything is okay now, he reassured himself. School had been shaky at the beginning. During the first couple of weeks, he'd tried to change his dorky image, disguising himself as a Cool Guy. He'd nearly killed himself pretending to be an expert in-line skater, and he had gotten into some embarrassing predicaments by telling outrageous lies about himself. He also had stopped wearing his glasses, and without them, he could only guess at what might be going on just ten feet in front of his face.

Jerry had eventually decided that it was much more fun being on the sixth-grade science team, where he could hang out with people who enjoyed the same things he did. He'd put his glasses back on; it was a relief to see everything clearly again.

When Jerry arrived at school, he found Brenda McAdams standing next to the big oak near the entrance to the building. She was talking with Kim and Kat Henley, identical twin sisters. Brenda smiled and waved him over.

"Hey, Flack," Brenda said. "Rumor has it that class elections are going to be held in a few weeks. We've discussed it, and we think you would make a great class president."

Jerry gawked at her. "Me? President of the sixth grade?"

"Sure, why not?" Kim Henley asked, shrugging. Her mane of fuzzy brown hair rocked back and forth like cotton candy in a breeze. "You're smart, you're nice, and you'd make a good leader."

"But I'm not . . ." He didn't want to say it.

"Popular?" asked Kat. "Handsome? Athletic? So what? We hate the Beautiful People. Don't ask me why, but most kids would rather not vote for a snob for student government. Popular, beautiful, and athletic equals snobby."

Kim rolled her eyes. "There you go again, generalizing. Lots of popular, good-looking, athletic kids aren't snobs."

"Oh, yeah?" asked Kat. "Name two."

"Well, at this precise moment, I can't think of any, smarty-pants," Kim said. "But by the end of the day, I'll have a whole list for you."

"I'm eager to see it," Kat said.

"Well," said Brenda, cutting in on the sisters' argument, "I think it's a great idea for you to run for president, Jerry. We'll be your campaign team."

"Why me?" Jerry asked. "You'd make a great president, Bren. Why don't *you* run?"

Brenda shrugged. "I'm more of a behind-the-scenes person. You'd be a better leader."

Jerry considered that. He'd never been a leader before, except maybe the day he helped his team win the sixth-grade science competition. He'd certainly been a leader then, and that had only been a few days ago. Maybe some latent leadership skills inside him were worming their way to the surface.

Jerry gazed at the swarm of students standing around the school grounds. "But I don't know a lot of the sixth graders," he said. "I only know the kids in my classes. And some of them I don't know very well."

"Don't worry about it," Brenda said. "That'll be our job. We'll put up posters and get out the word about you and your platform."

"My platform?" Jerry asked.

"You have to have a platform," Kim said. "You know, the stuff you stand for."

"What you want to do as president," Kat explained.

"What *would* you do if you were president?" Brenda asked.

Jerry thought a moment. "Well, I've thought it would be really cool if we could get e-mail stations in the lunchroom."

"Wow," Kim and Kat said in unison.

Brenda's eyes opened wide. "That would be so cool."

"And wouldn't it be great to have more parties just for the sixth grade?" he suggested.

"Yeah!" Brenda said. "Everyone would like that idea."

Jerry grinned. He was on a roll now. "And I think it would be good if the sixth grade had our own common room. You know, a meeting place where we could hang out before and after school."

"What did I tell you?" Brenda said, grinning at Kim and Kat. "He's the perfect choice for president."

Jerry smiled as he considered the possibility. Jerry Flack, president of the sixth grade. It sounded wonderful. Maybe he should run for president. The bad dream had been about his rotten past in elementary school. That was then; this is now. He'd been accepted at Hawthorne Middle School. He could do whatever he wanted to do. The world was his oyster.

The bell rang, and crowds of students headed for the school entrance.

"So, you'll think about it?" Brenda asked as they walked toward the door.

"Yeah," Jerry said. "I'll think about it."

But he'd already decided. He was ready for the challenge. "Jerry Flack, president," had a special ring to it. That had to mean something.

Maybe something wonderful.

Chapter Two

Jerry stopped at his locker and reached for the combination lock. Right 66, left 32, right 5. No problem.

He smiled to himself as he yanked open the locker door. Jerry Flack, presidential candidate, knows his locker combination.

"Hey, Jer." Craig Fox leaned against the next locker.

Jerry instinctively touched his glasses. He didn't really expect Craig to grab them, but enough of the dream still clung to Jerry that he felt a little nervous.

"You see the new girl?" Craig asked. "She came

yesterday. I happened to be talking to Mr. Meyer when she walked into the office."

Mr. Meyer was the assistant principal. Jerry wasn't surprised that Craig had been "talking to" Mr. Meyer, although he thought it was more likely that Mr. Meyer was talking to *him*. Jerry wondered what kind of trouble Craig had gotten himself into this time.

"What new girl?" Jerry asked. He slid the books that he'd used for homework onto the top shelf and pulled out his language arts and social studies books for his morning classes.

Craig poked him with a sharp elbow. "Over there, Flack. With the weird short hair."

Jerry rubbed his arm where Craig had jabbed him and looked across the hall. Craig was right; the girl's hair was very short. In fact, it wasn't much longer than Jerry's. And it was a weird color. The only thing Jerry could think of that was similar to the shiny red-brown of this girl's hair was their dining room table. Jerry had never seen a person with mahogany-colored hair.

"Unusual hair color," Jerry said.

Craig snorted. "That's not her *real* hair color."

"How can you tell?"

"The roots, man. Look at the roots. They're sort of light brown."

Jerry gazed at the girl again. "Oh, yeah," he said.

The girl slumped against a locker. Jerry could see a large wad of purple gum rolling around in her mouth as she chewed.

"I heard she's from Hollywood," Craig said.

"California?"

"No, numbskull, Hollywood, Alaska." Craig laughed hoarsely. "Of *course*, Hollywood, C-A."

Jerry drew himself up. "Yeah, so?"

"So her father works in the movie business, man!" Craig said. "She knows all kinds of big stars. All the ones you see at the Academy Awards."

"Why is she here?" Jerry asked. "Spencer Lake is a long way from Hollywood."

"How should I know?" Craig said. "I ain't no gossip columnist."

"Well, how'd you know she was from Hollywood?" Jerry asked.

"'Cause I *eavesdropped*, man," Craig said. "She was in the office, talking to the secretaries, droppin' names all over the place. You should've seen Mrs. Bruin's eyes. They nearly popped out of her head." He gazed off. "I wish they had popped out; that would've been cool."

Jerry rolled his eyes. "See you, Fox."

"Yeah," Craig said.

Jerry headed for his language arts class. Brenda was waiting for him at the classroom door.

"Hey, Jerry, look." She pointed to a poster on the wall across the hall.

RUN FOR CLASS OFFICE

Represent Your Class on the Student Council

Nomination papers available in the office

ELECTIONS HELD SEPTEMBER 22ND

"I really think you should run," Brenda said.

"Yeah, it could be fun," Jerry agreed.

Brenda's face opened into a big smile. "Are you saying yes? You've decided to run?"

"Yeah," Jerry said. "It'd be good to get some new things going at Hawthorne."

"Great!" Brenda said. "I'll get together with Kim and Kat. We'll recruit a few more people and get going on the campaign. We've just got two weeks before the election."

Students were filing past them into the language arts classroom. Jerry and Brenda trailed behind a group of kids and sat at their desks in the front.

The new girl with short mahogany hair appeared at the classroom door and walked in with Ms. Robertson, just as the late bell rang.

"Good morning," Ms. Robertson said to the class. "We have a new student. This is Zoey Long. Zoey, there's an extra seat in the back corner. Why don't you sit there for now?"

Zoey shambled back to her seat and slumped into the chair.

Jerry heard a buzz of girls' voices behind him.

"Hollywood," one of the girls said, her voice loud enough to carry.

"Are you really from Hollywood?" Cinnamon O'Brien asked, leaning around another student to see Zoey.

Zoey didn't even look in Cinnamon's direction. "Yeah."

"Have you ever met Drew Barrymore? Or—how about Britney Spears?"

Zoey sighed loudly and lazily turned toward Cinnamon. "Sure. They've been to parties at my house."

"Wow!"

"Are you kidding?"

"That's so *cool*!"

Excited voices filled the classroom.

"Imagine," Zoey said, her voice expressionless. The class became immediately silent. "They even drank out of our glasses and used our bathroom."

Giggles and murmurs bubbled up around the room.

"Well, Zoey, welcome to Hawthorne Middle School," Ms. Robertson said, smiling.

Ms. Robertson was one of Jerry's favorite teachers. She was small and pretty, and she sponsored the sixth-grade science team, along with Mr. Hooten, the science teacher. "I'm sure you'll make friends quickly and enjoy it here."

Zoey shrugged.

"Well," Ms. Robertson said, turning to the rest of the class, "I hope you all noticed the poster on the wall across from our classroom. The sixth grade needs class officers—"

The door opened, and Gabe Marshall loped in. Snickers came from the back of the room. Gabe looked over at his admirers and grinned.

"Do you have a late pass?" Ms. Robertson asked him.

"Nope. I was talking to somebody about the game Saturday, and we lost track of time." He continued to grin. "Sorry."

"I'm glad you're sorry, Gabe," Ms. Robertson said. "But you're still late. You'll have to come in after school."

Gabe's eyes widened in surprise. "But I was only like sixty seconds late."

"Late is late," Ms. Robertson said. "I'll see you after school."

Gabe's followers laughed again as he strode to his seat in the back, treating them to a small smile. Like a prince among the peons, Jerry thought. Gabe loved the limelight.

"As I was saying," Ms. Robertson said, "we need candidates for student council, and I hope someone from this class runs. We have some very capable students in here."

"What do you do if you want to run?" Cinnamon O'Brien grinned self-consciously and glanced at the friends surrounding her.

"Are you going to run?" Robin Hedges asked her.

"I'm just asking a question," Cinnamon said. She tilted her head in a coy pose and smiled at Gabe. Jerry could picture her practicing that pose in front of a mirror, angling her head to look as cute as possible.

Cinnamon O'Brien was arguably the prettiest girl in the sixth grade. She had long red hair that tumbled down her back in large waves, a tiny button nose, and big blue eyes, the kind that heroines always have in Disney's animated movies.

Jerry had had a crush on Cinnamon when school first started. But he realized, after being around Cinnamon for a while, that she wasn't his type, and he liked Brenda a lot better. Besides, Cinnamon was interested in other things. Gabe Marshall, for instance.

"I think Gabe should run," Cinnamon said. "He's so popular, he could become president of the sixth grade."

Jerry's hands suddenly became clammy.

Brenda, sitting in front of Jerry, turned in her seat and out the corner of her mouth whispered, "She's got to be kidding. *Gabe Marshall* on student government? What a nightmare."

"Running for a class office isn't about popularity," Ms. Robertson said. "It's about helping Hawthorne be the best school it can be. It's about service to your class."

"Right," Brenda murmured.

"Whatever," Cinnamon said. "I still think Gabe should run."

Gabe grinned at Cinnamon. "Hey, maybe I *should* run for president. I could get some things changed around here. Like the late rules."

That got a big laugh from his friends. Jerry noticed that some of the girls looked over at the corner of the room to get Zoey's reaction. She wasn't paying attention. She slouched in her chair and examined her nails, which were covered with a deep green fingernail polish.

"So what do you have to do to run?" Gabe asked.

Jerry was close enough to see Ms. Robertson's jaw tighten. "Well, Gabe, if student government appeals to you, you'll need to go to the office and fill out a nomination paper."

"I'll get it for you, Gabe," Cinnamon said.

"Okay, cool," Gabe said. "Bring it to me at lunch."

Now Jerry felt a sinking sensation in his chest. If he ran for class president, he was going to have to run against Gabe Marshall, the most popular guy in the whole sixth grade. Sure, Gabe was a lousy candidate for student government—Jerry couldn't imagine anything good that would be accomplished during a Gabe Marshall administration—but would the students take that into consideration when they voted?

Jerry looked around the classroom and saw grins on the faces of at least ten people who apparently thought it would be fun to have Gabe heading the sixth grade.

Maybe I shouldn't run, Jerry thought. Maybe the battle's been lost before it's been fought. How could he possibly win more votes than Gabe?

Brenda leaned backward toward Jerry and mumbled, "Don't worry, Flack. The sixth graders aren't stupid. They'll realize you're the best candidate for president. We'll win in a landslide."

Jerry nodded. When Brenda turned back toward the front of the class, he let out a quiet sigh.

It wasn't too late to tell Brenda he'd changed his mind. He could easily tell her that he'd decided to concentrate on other cool things, like spending time with his friends and working on the science team. She would understand. She was a good friend and wanted the best for him.

He'd tell her at lunch. Jerry felt relief flood through his body.

It sure was a good thing he hadn't told anyone besides Brenda that he wanted to be president. He wouldn't lose face with her.

He knuckled his glasses back up on the bridge of his nose and turned his attention to Ms. Robertson, who he suddenly realized had started class.

This would be no problem.

Chapter Three

"That new girl, Zoey, sure looks bored," Brenda said. "Or unhappy." She walked along the hall with Jerry, heading to lunch.

"Yeah," Jerry said. But he wasn't thinking about Zoey Long or how bored she had acted in class. He was waiting for the best time to break the news to Brenda that he wouldn't run for class president.

"I guess Spencer Lake seems like the end of the world after going to parties with famous movie stars," Brenda said. "I heard that Zoey's parents got a divorce, and her mother moved back here to be near her family. I think Mrs. Long grew up somewhere nearby."

"Yeah," Jerry said. He took a big breath. Now

was the time. "Brenda, I've changed my mind. I guess I won't run for president."

"What!" Brenda cried and stopped in the middle of the hall. "But you said you wanted to run."

Students just behind Brenda bumped into her, but she didn't seem to notice. The kids began flowing around her, like water gushing around a log in a stream. Jerry grabbed Brenda's arm and pulled her to the lockers to get her out of the way.

"What changed your mind?"

"Well, I think I'd just rather spend my time hanging out with you guys on the science team."

Brenda frowned. "But Kim and Kat and Chad and Tony and I are all *on* the science team. I already asked Kim and Kat if they want to campaign for you. They were going to see the others and ask them, too. Listen, we'll be hanging out together, but working on your campaign. It'll be fun."

"I don't want to," Jerry said. He had to nip this in the bud right now. Already too many people knew that he had been interested in running.

Brenda gazed at him. "You're worried you can't beat Gabe Marshall," she said. "Right?"

Jerry shrugged.

"Well, you're wrong. Gabe may not be totally brain-dead, but he sure acts like it. What sixth grader would want him to lead our class?"

"I could name quite a few, actually," Jerry said.

"Maybe a handful of kids, the people who are

constantly late to class," Brenda said. "But everyone else will think Gabe is stupid if he uses that in his platform."

"Well, I still don't want to run," Jerry said. "Come on, let's go to the cafeteria and tell Kim and Kat before they tell anyone else."

They followed the crowd down to the cafeteria and found themselves entering the large room just behind Gabe Marshall and Craig Fox. Gabe was laughing and talking loudly to Craig.

"And there was this huge mountain of tomato soup cans, so we pulled out three cans from the bottom row, and the whole thing went crashing onto the floor. Oh, man, you should've seen the mess. Everybody came running from all over the store, and we just walked away, looking surprised, as if the cans fell all by themselves. It was so cool!"

Brenda shot Jerry a look and murmured, "This idiot wants to be president of our class?"

As Jerry moved into the cafeteria, he heard a rhythmic clapping from one corner. Brenda grabbed his arm and pointed to their lunch table, where Kim and Kat Henley stood, clapping. Chad Newsome and Tony Abbott stood on a bench at the table and pointed to Jerry in the throng of kids. All four chanted in loud voices.

"Jerry, Jerry, he's our man!
If he can't do it, nobody can!"

"Oh, no." Jerry was sweating.

"They've already started the campaign," Brenda said.

Dozens of heads in the cafeteria turned to gaze at Jerry. The Henley sisters, along with Chad and Tony, demonstrating that they had more than one chant in their repertoire, hollered another one.

> *Flack for president! He's our guy.*
> *There's no one better, and that's no lie.*

"Come on." Jerry gently pushed aside students standing in the way and hurried toward his chanting supporters.

"Jerry, are you running for sixth-grade president?" Cinnamon O'Brien stepped from the crowd and planted herself in his path. Gabe appeared next to her a second later, a scowl contorting his face.

"Yeah, Flack," Gabe said. "Are you running, too?" His scowl faded, and his lips curled into a malicious grin. "Hey, you know, that could be interesting."

Jerry's pulse quickened. "Well, I haven't really decided yet," he said. He forced a smile back at Gabe. "I guess my friends are trying to convince me."

"Jerry has some great ideas for the sixth grade, so a lot of us think he should run," Brenda added.

Students gathered around them to listen.

"I got some great ideas, too," Gabe said. He stood up straighter and puffed out his chest.

Cinnamon grinned. "Gabe wants to change the late rules at Hawthorne."

"Yeah, but there's more stuff than that I want to change," Gabe said.

"Like what?" Brenda asked.

"Like, if you have to go to detention, you shouldn't have to do homework," Gabe said. "You should be able to talk to the other kids and play video games and stuff." He surveyed the crowd around him and raised his voice. "I bet Meyer thinks video games are a waste of time. But he's wrong. They help us improve our eye-hand coordination."

Brenda rolled her eyes.

Gabe turned to Jerry. "Yeah, I think you should run, Flack."

Jerry's body stiffened, and his knees felt a little quivery. Gabe was obviously convinced he could beat Jerry, or he'd never encourage the competition.

Brenda's eyes narrowed. "Even if Gabe becomes president of the sixth grade, he couldn't get video games into the detention room. Or change the late rules."

Gabe shrugged. "I've been thinking about it. If I got elected president, I don't think Meyer would do much to me if I'm late to classes. He wouldn't want to punish a class president, 'cause the president's supposed to be like this perfect kid, you know? It would make the whole school look bad."

Some of the eavesdropping students laughed.

"Besides," Cinnamon said, giggling and turning to the audience surrounding them, "the rank of assistant principal isn't that much higher than sixth-grade president."

"Oh, brother," Brenda muttered.

Jerry gazed at Gabe—who was still grinning at the idea of intimidating Mr. Meyer—and tried not to imagine him as the leader of their class. It was unthinkable that he might win the presidency and use his position for nothing more than helping out the students who disrupt everyone else. The sixth grade at Hawthorne Middle School deserved better than that.

"I think you're right," Jerry said to Gabe.

"I am?" Gabe's look of surprise dissolved into suspicion. "About what?"

"I think I should run for sixth-grade president," Jerry said. "I'd like to do some cool things for the kids in our class."

He was aware of Brenda's bounce of happiness beside him. "*Yes*," she whispered.

In one moment, several emotions flashed across Gabe's face: surprise, worry, then finally, amusement.

"Cool, Flack," Gabe said, nodding his head thoughtfully. "We'll see who gets the most votes."

Cinnamon giggled again. "Hey, you guys, this'll be fun. Like Miss America, only you don't have to wear special outfits."

Brenda set her jaw. "This isn't a beauty contest, Cinnamon," she said. "Or a popularity contest. This is about who will do the best job representing the class."

"Right," Gabe said, grinning as if he had his win already sewn up.

Jerry gazed at Gabe and wondered. Would the rest of his class vote for the best candidate? Or would they just vote for the most popular guy? Or the best looking?

Jerry hoped he'd made the right decision. He took in a deep breath. He'd find out soon enough.

"Is it done yet?" Melissa called from the ground below.

She sat on the grass, wrestling with their terrier spaniel, Sassy. Sassy loved playing with an old knotted piece of rope that was beginning to unravel. She'd thrown the thing, soggy with doggy spit, down near Melissa's feet and barked, demanding a game of tug-of-war.

Sassy growled, her tail wagging, and Melissa growled back.

"Almost done," Jerry's dad answered. He turned to Jerry, who was standing in the tree house next to him. "Hammer on this last rail, and we've got her done."

While his dad held the board, Jerry hammered it solidly into place. "Hey, Melissa," he called, peering at her over the rail. "You can come up now."

"*All right!*" Melissa dropped the dog's rope, rushed to the ladder, climbed up, and stepped into her tree house.

She walked to the center and turned around in a full circle, her eyes wide. "Oh!" she breathed. "It's *beautiful* up here. I can practically see forever!"

Jerry grinned. "Well, at least down to the corner."

"The roof will keep out the rain and some of the blowing leaves," their dad said.

"I'm going to stay up here all the time," Melissa said. "Maybe I'll even *sleep* up here."

Mr. Flack's eyebrows shot up. "Well, we'll see about that."

Melissa frowned. "There's that 'we'll see' thing again." She turned to her brother. "Jerry, do you think—?"

"Not a chance," he said.

Her lower lip jutted out. "That's what I thought."

"But think how much fun you'll have up here in the daytime," Jerry said.

Melissa brightened. "Yeah! I'm going to call Rachel over right now." She scrambled for the ladder.

"Be careful," her dad warned. "Slow down."

"I will."

Jerry and his dad collected the tools that were scattered around the tree house floor and stored them away in the toolbox.

"Jerry?" his mother called from the back door. "Telephone."

"Be right there."

He climbed down the ladder and hurried into the house.

"Hey, Flack," Brenda said after he'd answered.

Jerry grinned at the sound of Brenda's voice. Even though she was his girlfriend (Jerry had even kissed her twice), Brenda called him by his last name. He liked that. He'd decided that—not counting a few kisses here and there—he wasn't ready for a major mushy relationship anyway. Brenda was his best buddy and favorite companion and, in his opinion, everything a girlfriend should be.

"Hey, Bren."

"I just wanted to tell you again that you made the right decision about running for president."

Jerry's stomach jumped. "I hope so."

"Say," Brenda said, "we have to start thinking about your campaign speech."

"What speech?"

"When I went to pick up the nomination paper for you, I got another sheet that says you have to give a two-minute speech in two weeks, just before the voting."

Jerry groaned. "I hate speeches."

"Well, try and get over it, Flack," Brenda said, "because this'll be in front of the entire sixth grade."

Now his stomach executed an impressive pirouette. "Are you serious?"

"Yes, indeedy. I think we should come up with something fun and different. We'll practice it until you can do it in your sleep."

"Sounds good to me," Jerry said, but he wasn't at all sure that he really meant it.

"Don't worry," Brenda said. "We've got a great team. You're going to wow 'em, Flack."

Jerry sighed. "I hope so."

They said good-bye, and Jerry hung up the phone. He stared at the kitchen wall, his hand still clutching the receiver. A speech? In front of the entire sixth-grade class?

"You okay, Jerry?"

Jerry's mind snapped to attention, and he turned to his mother, releasing his grip on the phone. "Uh, yeah," he said.

But he wondered if he really was okay. What had he gotten himself into? Running against popular Gabe Marshall? Giving a speech in front of nearly a hundred kids?

This was already turning into a nightmare.

Chapter Four

"Jerry, take a step that way." Cinnamon waved her hand to the side.

Jerry stepped sideways. "What's the matter?"

Jerry and Brenda stood in the hall a few feet from his locker. Cinnamon leaned against the locker next to his and stared across the hall, her view now cleared.

"I'm watching Zoey," Cinnamon said, her voice low. "She's so cool."

Jerry glanced over at Zoey's locker. It was closed, and the mahogany-haired girl slumped against it, her arms folded.

"She looks bored," Brenda said.

"Yeah, that's what I *mean*," Cinnamon said, her

eyes brightening. "It's like she's so cool, *everything* bores her." She sighed. "It would be so great to be that cool. I wish I could hang out with her." She scowled like Zoey and collapsed against the locker, becoming a mirror image of the girl across the hall.

Jerry tried not to smile, and Brenda shook her head.

"How do you think my hair would look really, really short?" Cinnamon asked.

"If you cut your hair," Brenda said, "you'd be cutting off your best feature."

"Hmm, I guess you're right," Cinnamon said, combing her luxurious locks with her fingers.

"Why don't you go over and talk to her?" Jerry suggested.

"Really?" Cinnamon straightened up, considering the possibility. "I hadn't thought of that."

"Yeah, what a concept," Brenda said. "Actually talking to a person to become friends. It might catch on."

"What should I say?" Cinnamon asked.

"Whatever you'd say to your other friends," Jerry said.

A light came into Cinnamon's eyes. "I could tell her about cheerleading tryouts. They're next week."

"Uh, maybe not," Brenda said, with a quick glance at Jerry. "Something tells me Zoey isn't the clapping and jumping type."

Cinnamon's smile faded. "Oh, yeah."

"Maybe you could offer to show her around," Jerry said. "You know, introduce her to your friends."

Cinnamon stared at Jerry a moment. She blinked. "No offense, Jerry, but that's really dorky. Hey, but maybe I could do it, only just not *tell* her that's what I'm going to do."

Jerry shrugged. "Whatever works."

Cinnamon took a big breath, straightened her shoulders, then realized what she was doing and sagged into a slouch. "Okay, guess I'll go talk to her now. Maybe I'll tell her about the sixth-grade ice-skating party on Friday."

"Uh—" Brenda started to speak, but Jerry interrupted her.

"Good luck."

Jerry and Brenda watched Cinnamon shuffle over to Zoey.

"I don't think Zoey's the ice-skating type either," Brenda murmured.

"Maybe not," Jerry said, "but Zoey has to respond to *something*."

Zoey, across the hall, turned to Cinnamon with no change of expression. Cinnamon said something, and Zoey shrugged. Cinnamon said something else, and Zoey shook her head. Cinnamon frowned and headed back to Jerry.

She scowled and her eyes narrowed. "Great idea to *talk* to her, Jerry," she growled. She turned on her heel and marched off.

"What did I do?" Jerry asked Brenda.

"You gave helpful advice that would've worked on anyone but Zoey," Brenda said. "Apparently, Zoey isn't an ice-skating enthusiast. But speaking of the skating party, I've been meaning to mention that. We should go."

"I'm not exactly an ice-skater," Jerry said.

"No problem," Brenda said. "You don't have to skate. It's like the swimming pool in the summertime. Lots of kids just lie in the sun looking cool, never putting a toe in the water, and nobody even notices. We'll sit around and drink Cokes and talk to people. Really, Flack, you should at least show up for the party. It would be good for the campaign."

"Well, I guess if I don't actually have to skate, it would be okay," Jerry said.

Brenda grinned. "Great. Come on, we don't want to be late for class."

Ms. Robertson came into the classroom and closed the door behind her as the bell rang, starting first period.

"Hey, Ms. Robertson," Robin called out. "The two people running for sixth-grade president are in this class."

Ms. Robertson smiled. "Yes, the nomination papers were delivered to my mailbox this morning. Good luck to you both, Jerry and Gabe. Do you have campaign managers and helpers?"

Jerry nodded. "Brenda's my manager, and we've got friends to help."

"Good." Ms. Robertson looked toward the back of the room. "How about you, Gabe?"

Gabe sat back in his seat, grinning. "Yeah, I guess Cinnamon's my manager. Right, Cinn?"

Jerry turned and looked back at Cinnamon. She sat slumped in her chair, her arms folded. She peeked over at Zoey, apparently to see if the girl had noticed. But Zoey was staring out the window.

"Cinnamon?" asked Ms. Robertson. "Are you running Gabe's campaign?"

Cinnamon lifted her shoulders in a lazy shrug. "I dunno," she said, as if she couldn't care less. "I guess so."

Ms. Robertson's eyebrows lifted. "Well, remember, you'll need to establish your platform, so students know what you stand for. You can put up posters, and you'll each make a speech just before the voting."

"So who's running for vice president?" asked Scott Perkins from the middle of the room. "And secretary?"

"Anyone who is interested," answered Ms. Robertson.

Cinnamon, forgetting her pose as bored sixth-grader and Zoey's clone, sat up and gazed over at Zoey. "Maybe Zoey would like to run."

Zoey snorted. "As if."

"No, I really, really mean it!" Cinnamon enthused. "It would be so cool to get someone from Hollywood on the student council!"

"Yeah, she could run for vice president with me," Gabe said. "And we could get movie stars to—you know, say they're for us. Just like in real politics."

"Yeah!" Cinnamon exclaimed. "Do you think Leonardo DiCaprio would—"

"Get real," Zoey said. "Leo's a little busy, if you know what I mean."

"Well, maybe some other movie star. How about—"

"No," Zoey said.

"Not even—"

Zoey stared hard at Cinnamon. "Which part of *no* didn't you understand?"

Cinnamon's face fell. "You mean, you don't want to be vice president?"

"Unthinkable as it is," Zoey said, "I can't imagine anything I'd rather *not* be."

"How about president?" Cinnamon tried once more.

Zoey shot her a withering look.

"Hey—" Gabe said, frowning. "That's my job."

"Not yet, it isn't," Brenda murmured.

Ms. Robertson held up her hand. "I think it works better if the person runs because she wants the challenge and responsibility," she said.

"Yeah," Gabe said with a big grin. "That's why I'm running."

"Riiight," Brenda murmured in Jerry's direction.

An idea flashed in Jerry's mind. He leaned forward and gently poked Brenda's shoulder.

"Think website," he whispered. She frowned, not understanding. "I could put up a website about my campaign."

Brenda's eyes grew big. "Brilliant!" she whispered. "We'll advertise it on posters. Everybody'll want to check it out!"

They grinned at each other.

This just might be fun, Jerry thought. Gabe would never think of using a website for his campaign.

Maybe running for president wouldn't be a nightmare after all.

"Is it ready?" Brenda asked. She scratched Sassy's neck.

"Almost." Jerry put down the shovel and kneeled next to Brenda in a corner of the Flacks' vegetable garden. The late afternoon sun felt warm on Jerry's face as he patted the mound of dirt that rose up before them.

"Looks like a volcano to me," Brenda said.

Jerry grinned and pushed his glasses back up on his nose. "Just wait till it erupts." He picked up the paper sack next to him and looked around. "I wish

Melissa were here. She loves science tricks."

Just then, the gate leading to the backyard opened and Melissa walked through. Behind her shuffled another girl, much younger than Jerry, but older than Melissa. She wore blue jeans and a T-shirt. Her brown hair was cut short around her ears, which made the diamond earrings that dangled above her shoulders all the more startling.

"Hey, Melissa," Jerry called. "Want to see a volcano erupt?"

"Oh, that's okay," Melissa said, waving her hand in a dismissive gesture. "I'm going to show Cory my tree house."

"What volcano?" Cory asked, walking around Melissa to the garden.

"Oh, it's just one of my brother's dumb tricks," Melissa said, trailing along behind Cory.

"Hey, there's a bottle under that dirt," Cory said. "I can see the top of it."

"Right," Jerry said. "We buried it and built up the mountain around it."

"Cool," Cory said. She flipped her earrings around with her fingers, and the diamonds flashed in the sunlight. "So when does it erupt?"

"As soon as I add the right ingredients," Jerry said.

He pulled a bottle of liquid detergent out of the sack and squirted about a tablespoon into the mouth of the bottle at the top of the volcano. Then he added a few drops of red food coloring. "The color makes it look authentic," Jerry said. "Molten lava is red hot."

Out of the sack, he took a bottle of vinegar and a glass measuring cup. He poured one cup of the vinegar into the mouth of the volcano.

"And now," Jerry said dramatically, rising to his feet. He lowered his voice to a whisper and added, "Stand back for the fiery inferno. Hold on to Sassy, Brenda."

Brenda held Sassy close.

Cory took a backward step and watched wide-eyed. Melissa watched Cory's reaction and did the same.

Jerry added two tablespoons of baking soda mixed with a little water into the opening at the top.

In a moment, the volcano erupted, red foam bubbling and belching from the top. For a full minute, the "molten lava" rushed down the mountain of dirt and puddled in a widening circle at Jerry's feet.

Sassy's ears flattened on top of her head and she barked, bobbing frantically up and down in Brenda's arms.

"She's afraid of the volcano," Brenda said, and Jerry patted her head.

"That's so cool!" Cory said. "Do it again."

"Yeah, do it again, Jerry," Melissa repeated.

"Nope," Jerry said. "A good performer always

leaves his audience wanting more."

"Oh, spit!" Cory said.

"What'd you say? *Spit?*" Melissa asked. She laughed. "That's funny. Oh, spit."

"Jerry, that was spectacular," Brenda said, still holding the squirming Sassy. "You should've given the science team a demonstration today. Where did you find that experiment?"

Jerry shrugged and grinned. "From a book at the library."

"Come on, Cory." Melissa tapped the girl's shoulder. "I'll show you the tree house."

"Hey, who's your friend?" Jerry asked his sister as they turned to go.

"Cory Brown," Melissa said, and she added with the utmost respect, "She's a third grader."

"Nice earrings," Brenda said.

"Thanks," Cory said. "I took 'em for show-and-tell."

Jerry smiled. "How did you and Melissa—?"

But Cory had turned to see the tree house and was already running toward it.

"Hey, wait, Cory!" Melissa called, taking off after her. "I'll show you how to get up there."

But Cory didn't wait to be shown. She scrambled up the ladder and jumped into the tree house.

"Wow! Cool!" she shrieked. "I can see for miles!"

Melissa had followed close behind and now stood next to Cory in the tree house, grinning. "What'd I tell ya?" she said. "Isn't it *great*?"

Cory hollered, "Hey, everybody! I'm Tarzan!"

"Yeah, I'm Tarzan!" Melissa yelled.

Brenda gazed at the girls in the tree. "Tarzan accessorizes with diamonds. Interesting."

Jerry laughed.

"And did you notice," Brenda said thoughtfully, turning back to Jerry, "that the element of drama that you'd normally get with diamond earrings is somehow lost when they're dangling from the ears of a third grader?"

"I had noticed that, yes," Jerry said. "But they've got to be fake diamonds. Her mother would never let her wear real diamonds out of the house."

"Let's hope so."

The sun shone over Brenda's shoulder and Jerry gazed at her, squinting.

"So, Bren," Jerry said, sitting on the lawn next to the garden, "you like the idea of starting a website for the campaign?" He scratched Sassy, who was calm now and sitting in the grass with her tongue lolling out of her mouth.

"Yes, indeedy," Brenda said, joining him on the grass. "I bet no kid running for class office at Hawthorne has ever put up a website. It's brilliant!"

"Thanks," Jerry said.

"We'll need a picture of you," Brenda suggested. "You have any good ones?"

"I have one that's okay."

"Great."

"And we can list the things I want to do if I get elected," Jerry said. "You know, the stuff in my platform."

"And maybe some information about you. Your interests, your family, where you came from. That kind of thing."

"Interests?" Jerry looked at her skeptically. "Like the science team?"

"Sure," Brenda said. "That's an important extracurricular activity. Besides, it shows you're smart."

Jerry frowned. "But what if the sixth graders don't want smart? What if they want popular?"

Brenda gazed at Jerry a moment. "I know, you're thinking about Gabe Marshall again." Jerry shrugged. "Look, let's face it, he's gorgeous. But Jerry, good looks can only take a person so far. After that, you need brains, talent, and people skills. And you've got all those things going for you."

Jerry was incredulous. "You think I have people skills?"

"Sure," Brenda said, surprised. "Don't *you*?"

Jerry thought about the time he felt so self-conscious about seeing a girl from his class at the public library, he tripped over his own feet and fell flat on his face in front of the circulation desk. And then there was the time he was so startled that a cool guy in his class said hi to him, he accidentally inhaled some spit and coughed so hard, a teacher sent for the school nurse. There was also that day when he had to interview his grandmother for a class project, but he got so flustered while he reorganized his questions, she got impatient and left. His own *grandmother*.

But those things happened last year at his old school. Jerry had matured quite a lot since then. He could talk to almost anybody without looking obviously nervous.

So maybe that was it. He hadn't matured all that much; he just knew how to hide his insecurities better.

"Well, I don't know . . ." he said.

"Listen," Brenda said with confidence, "you're going to be the next sixth-grade president, and I'm not going to listen to anything different."

"Okay," Jerry said. "Thanks, Bren."

A series of shrieks came from the tree house. Cory had seen someone on the sidewalk and was waving. "Hey, you fourth-grade idiot!" she yelled. "Look up here! Hi! We've got our very own *tree house*!"

Melissa laughed, "Yeah, you jerk! And you can't come up here! It's just for *us*."

"Ha Ha!" hollered Cory.

"Hey!" Jerry called sharply. "Cut it out up there. Melissa, you know better than that."

"Oh, Jerry! Leave us alone." Melissa waved her

arm angrily. But she looked embarrassed, and Jerry realized she'd forgotten that he and Brenda were still in the yard.

"Cory's not exactly a good influence on Melissa," Jerry said. "I ought to send her home."

"Oh, they're okay," Brenda said. "Melissa's probably just impressed that a third grader would want to play with her." She grinned. "A third grader with diamonds."

"Yeah, I guess you're right," Jerry said. He got up and brushed the grass off his jeans. "Come on," he said, "let's go start on our website."

"Yeah," Brenda answered. "It'll be so impressive, it'll blow Gabe right out of the water."

That sounded awfully good to Jerry. But then he decided he'd be happy with just not letting Gabe blow *him* out of the water.

Chapter Five

Brenda emerged from the crowd milling around the rink at Skate Land.

"Here's your Coke and change," she said, setting the coins and cup of soda on the small table in front of Jerry. She leaned down and whispered, "It's a great excuse for staying off the ice."

"Thanks," Jerry said. "Three people have already said, 'Come skate with us.'"

"As long as you have a Coke in your hand, you don't need to skate," Brenda said, plopping into the chair across from Jerry. "Just hold it up, shake your head, and smile."

"Okay."

A current pop song blared from the loudspeaker

overhead, providing a handy rhythm to skate by for the kids on the ice. Jerry tapped his fingers on his cup in time to the music.

Brenda suddenly sat at attention and murmured, "Don't look now, but your opponent just arrived."

"With his entourage?"

"Yup. Cinnamon, Robin, and Craig."

"Just watch. Gabe will skate," Jerry predicted. "And he won't fall down and look stupid."

"So what?" Brenda said lightly. "You won't fall down and look stupid, either, because you're going to be too busy talking to people and sipping your Coke."

Jerry sighed. "I'm missing my favorite science show on TV tonight."

"Yeah," Brenda said, "but if you were at home watching it, you'd be missing out on this great opportunity to mingle with the voters." She saw someone over Jerry's shoulder, smiled and waved. "Hi, Jennifer. Hi, Sandi!"

"Yeah, I guess you're right."

"So put those great people skills of yours to work," Brenda said.

"Okay," he answered.

Brenda stared at him levelly. Her eyebrows went up.

"Oh. You mean now?" he asked.

She smiled. "Now would be good."

"Right." He saluted her with the Coke. "Here

goes." He got up, then turned back to Brenda. "So you really think I have people skills?"

"Truckloads."

Jerry considered that. "That might be over-stating it."

Brenda grinned. "Would you like me to come with you?"

"That's the best offer I've had all day. Come on."

Brenda laughed and stood up. "Hey, there's Kim and Kat. Let's start with some easy people."

"Great."

Kim saw them coming and waved. "Glad you two showed up."

"Yeah," Kat said. "We were just about to go out onto the ice. Wanna come with us?"

"No, we're going to hang around the tables for a while," Brenda said.

"Gabe Marshall's here," Kim said. "He walked by, and he smelled like Old Spice."

"Yeah, can you believe it?" Kat said. "He's not old enough to shave, but he wears aftershave."

"How do you know it was Old Spice?" Jerry asked.

"Oh, it was Old Spice, all right," Kim said. "Our brother uses it every morning, and the whole bathroom stinks after he leaves for school."

"Yeah, it's so strong, you walk in there and start coughing your head off," Kat said. "Gets in your nose, your throat, it's awful."

"He really overdoes it," Kim said.

Kat turned to Kim. "Why don't you tell him that?"

"That he overdoes the Old Spice?"

"Yeah."

"'Cause he might kill me. Why don't *you* tell him?"

"Why don't *you*?"

"I just told you. Besides, that's Mom's job."

"Oh, good idea. Tell her to tell him."

"Why don't *you* tell her?"

"Why don't *you*? It was your idea."

"Well, nice to see you guys," Brenda cut in. "Jerry and I are going to do some serious mingling now."

They hurried away.

"Do they ever agree on anything?" Jerry whispered when they were out of earshot of the sisters.

"Oh, sure," Brenda said. "Maybe once or twice a year. It's pretty shocking when it happens."

"Hey, Jerry!"

Jerry turned to see Cinnamon and Gabe at the entrance to the ice, next to the board and Plexiglas wall that separated the rink from the rest of the facility. They had already put on their skates.

"Come here!" Cinnamon called.

Jerry and Brenda strolled over to them. Gabe threw an arm over Cinnamon's shoulder.

"You and Brenda going to skate?" Cinnamon

asked. She giggled. "Gabe doesn't think you'll really get on the ice, Jerry."

Jerry's heart lunged, but he held up his Coke and realized with satisfaction that his hand didn't shake. "Maybe I will later."

"Sure, Flack," Gabe said. "Like I really believe that."

"You guys have a good time," Brenda called out as they skated away.

Jerry suddenly wished he could bolt out the door into the parking lot. Going to a skating party and not skating was going to be harder than he'd thought. Especially if Gabe gave him a hard time about it.

"Maybe I'll make the rounds and see everybody and then leave," Jerry told Brenda.

"Well, okay," Brenda said. "But let's give it a half hour, anyway. You can put off skating that long." She grinned. "Just don't drink your Coke too fast."

An unpleasant sensation settled in Jerry's stomach. It took a moment to realize what it was, and when he recognized it, he felt even worse: it was fear.

Let's face it, he thought. I'm a coward, a 'fraidy cat, a gutless wonder.

Just because he didn't want to skate.

Correction, Jerry thought. It was because he didn't want to *sprawl all over the ice in front of fifty kids.*

Was that so bad? He didn't think so. So then why did his stomach feel as if it were a cauldron filled with flesh-eating acid?

Chad and Tony appeared. "Hey, Brenda! Jerry!" Chad called. "Tony and I are going to start a chain. Come help us."

Jerry held up his Coke. "I'm working on a soda," he said. "Sorry." He tried to ignore the sour sensation in his stomach.

"Okay," Chad said. He turned to Tony. "Come on, we'll get it going ourselves."

They went through the entrance to the ice rink and waved to some of their friends.

"We might be the only people not skating in the chain after it gets going," Jerry murmured to Brenda.

"Don't worry, a lot of kids won't join," Brenda said.

Jerry realized he was breathing shallowly and gulped some air. Why had he agreed to come? Already Chad and Tony had waved over Kim and Kat and three other skaters. He'd heard of skating chains made of fifty or more people, all hooked up, each skater hanging on to the waist of the skater ahead. If all the sixth graders were in the chain, he and Brenda would look pretty conspicuous sitting at the table while he sipped his Coke.

"So how hard is it to skate in a chain?" Jerry murmured to Brenda.

"If the rest of the kids skate pretty well, they all hold you up," Brenda said. "Otherwise, it's a mess because the rest of the skaters pull you over. But it's still fun, even if you fall. Everybody piles on top of each other, and there's lots of laughing and screeching."

Jerry thought a second and swallowed hard. "Maybe I should try it."

"Really?" Brenda's eyes held more than a hint of surprise. "It's not nearly as scary as rollerblading down a killer hill, which you've already done. This way, the farthest you can fall is down on the ice, right in front of you."

"Right," Jerry said. How bad could it be? Maybe after he skated in the chain, he could get off the ice, and Gabe would leave him alone. "Let's do it."

"Great," Brenda said, grinning, her eyes wide. "Come on, we'll join the chain together."

Jerry's stomach felt a bit better, but now his heart was a big bass drum in his chest. He counted fifteen people in the chain behind Chad, with more skaters joining every second. Everyone looked as if they were having a great time. Jerry had to admit that it looked like fun. But then, they all knew how to skate.

Jerry and Brenda went to the skate-rental counter, found two pairs of skates in their sizes, went to chairs near the ice, and put them on.

"All set?" Brenda asked.

"One question," Jerry said, watching the line of skaters sail around the ice in one long, snakelike formation.

"What?"

"How do we get over to the skaters?"

"Oh. Well, normally if a person wants to skate in the chain, that person *skates* over to join it."

"That could be a problem."

"You'll be fine," Brenda said. "Here, take my hand."

They got up and walked on their blades to the rink entrance. Brenda flashed Jerry an encouraging smile and they inched onto the ice.

"We'll move out a little bit from the wall," Brenda said, "and they'll come around and pick us up."

Jerry wondered if that meant that the chain would slow down or even stop for them. He doubted that. He watched as Craig and Robin joined the line. The other skaters didn't stop, didn't slow down. In fact, they hardly seemed to notice that their line was getting longer and longer as more kids hooked on the end.

"Come on," Brenda said.

"What do we do first?" Jerry asked.

"Well, letting go of the wall would be a good start," Brenda said.

"Oh. Right." Jerry released his hold on the wall and balanced between his feet, which he'd placed shoulder-distance apart under him. He felt unsteady, as if he had no control of those feet which might slide out from under the rest of his body at any moment.

"Okay," Brenda said. "Now slowly transfer your weight between one foot and the other. Use the tips of your skates to push off gently."

Jerry, who had been listening carefully, did exactly as Brenda suggested. One foot first and then the next foot. He grinned. He had moved about five feet and hadn't fallen down.

"Good job," Brenda said. "Let's wave to the kids in the chain, so they'll come pick us up."

"Okay." Jerry stared at the ice, concentrating on staying upright.

Brenda waved at Chad, who was still leading the group.

"Okay, here they come. Oh-oh."

"What?" Jerry asked.

"Guess who just joined the chain?"

Jerry gazed up at the long line of skaters, now twenty-seven strong. Gabe and Cinnamon had just attached themselves to the end.

"What does that mean?" he asked. "I mean, if Gabe and Cinnamon are on the end?"

"Nothing, I hope," Brenda said.

Chad, at the front of the chain, passed close and grinned at Jerry and Brenda. "Hop on," he said.

"Slow down, okay?" Brenda murmured to him, and he nodded.

The speed of the chain slowed the tiniest bit. Brenda planted Jerry's two hands on her waist. "Hold on tight," she said, and she held her hand out to catch hold of Cinnamon's waist as the chain skated past.

Cinnamon came by in a blur. Jerry felt a sudden *whoosh* and he was jerked into movement. He gripped Brenda's waist, his legs stiff and locked at the knees.

Brenda glanced back under her arm. "Soften your knees!" she called back. "Move your feet like— like you're *skating*. You know."

All at once, Jerry realized that they weren't a part of the chain anymore. He, Brenda, Cinnamon, and Gabe were out on the middle of the ice, alone. The rest of the chain moved on.

"Why'd you let go?" Cinnamon asked Gabe, dropping her hands from his waist.

Jerry realized he was still hanging onto Brenda as if his life depended on it. Gabe skated around him, laughing, then took something out of the pocket of his shirt.

Jerry released his grip on Brenda and went sprawling forward on the ice. Landing on his stomach, he slid a few inches before coming to a stop.

Jerry saw a flash and looked up into the eye of a camera.

"Smile, Flack," Gabe said. He shot another picture of Jerry, who stared up at him, open mouthed.

"Get up. Let's see you skate."

"Cut it out, Gabe," Brenda said. "This is his first time on ice skates. Don't you have any sense of fair play?"

Fair play. Jerry figured that was probably a concept beyond Gabe's grasp.

Brenda skated over to him. "On your knees first, then one leg at a time," she murmured.

Jerry felt his cheeks burn fiercely as he pulled his knees under his body. He didn't think he could stand up without falling again, but he had to try.

"Come on, Gabe," Cinnamon said. "Let's get in the chain again."

"In a minute," Gabe said, grinning. "I want to record Flack's first time skating."

Jerry had one skate and one knee on the ice. "Now the left foot," Brenda whispered.

Jerry managed to get both blades on the ice. Slowly, unsteadily, he stood up.

"Good going, Flack!" Gabe said. "Now all you have to do is skate to the exit."

Brenda held out her hand, but Jerry, humiliated, waved her away. Remembering Brenda's earlier instructions, he gently pushed off with his left toe and, both legs wobbling, he began to skate. His face continued to burn, and he knew that his cheeks were streaked with the color of the beets growing in his mother's vegetable garden. He hated when that happened, when his whole face gave away how mortified he felt. It was as if his own *skin*, in which he'd lived for his entire life, had betrayed him.

He was thankful that Brenda had stopped defending him. He didn't want her help. He had to do this on his own.

He pushed gently with his right foot, and his left went out from under him. Once again, he found himself kissing the ice.

"Whoo! This is great!" Jerry heard the *click click* of Gabe's camera.

"Gabe!" Cinnamon shouted. "Stop that! So what if Jerry can't skate? Who *cares*?"

I care, Jerry thought. I care.

Slowly, Jerry made his way toward the exit door, which led off the ice. Gabe caught it all on film, chortling with satisfaction every time he captured Jerry flinging his arms out wildly to steady himself, every time his legs wobbled, every time he went down on one knee or two.

It took another two or three agonizing minutes for Jerry to reach the exit and clamber off the ice.

Gabe waved cheerfully at Jerry. "Hey, Flack, you can be very entertaining." He laughed. "Come on, Cinnamon." He and Cinnamon skated off toward the chain of kids.

With Brenda following, Jerry slumped into a chair and took off his skates.

"He's the biggest jerk I've ever known in my life," Brenda said. "That was unbelievably mean."

Jerry, who felt as if he'd swallowed a golf ball, didn't trust his voice to speak for a couple of minutes. Finally, he said, "At least the other kids weren't crowded around. They probably didn't notice. They were busy skating in the chain."

Brenda said, "Yeah," but Jerry knew she didn't believe it.

In fact, Jerry knew that they'd seen everything. The kids in the chain had skated past once, and nearly all of them were gawking at him. They saw Gabe taking pictures of him as he flailed away on the ice. Some were smiling, some were laughing, some just watched.

Jerry and Brenda walked silently to the skate-rental counter and returned their skates. Brenda called her mom to come pick them up. They pushed open the heavy doors leading to the parking lot and walked out into the crisp evening air.

Jerry's mind kept replaying over and over his humiliation on the ice. Each time, he felt more ashamed.

Brenda sat on a bench next to the entrance to Skate Land, but Jerry moved off into the parking lot. He didn't want to see any of the sixth graders who might be leaving early. He just hoped Brenda's mom would arrive soon.

"Jerry?" Brenda appeared at his side. "You want to come over and make a frozen pizza?"

"No."

"Popcorn?"

"No, thanks."

"Maybe playing a computer game would take your mind off—"

"No, I don't want to do that," Jerry said. "But I'll tell you what I do want."

"What?"

Jerry blew out a breath and straightened up tall. His jaw was tight, and when he spoke, his voice came out strong and low. "I want to get even."

Chapter Six

Monday at school, the pictures of Jerry sprawled all over the ice were making the rounds. Gabe had apparently made lots of copies, because everywhere Jerry turned, he saw sixth graders standing in huddles, looking at the pictures.

"Look at Flack's face!" he heard one sixth-grade boy exclaim, grinning. "His mouth is open so wide, he could swallow a softball."

"You should've seen him," a girl said, bending over the picture she held in her hand. "I felt so sorry for him! He looked totally miserable."

"I thought I'd die laughing," another girl said. "Oh, look, here he comes." She whisked the picture behind her back, but she didn't bother trying to hide the smirk on her face.

Jerry nodded to her. Let her laugh. He felt better now.

Brenda was waiting for Jerry at the door of their language arts classroom. She watched him walk toward her, and her eyes looked worried.

"You okay?" she murmured.

"I'm fine," he said. He even smiled at her. "I figured it out."

Brenda's eyes widened. "You did? You figured out how to get even with Gabe?"

He nodded. "I'll tell you later."

Brenda grinned and followed him into the classroom.

A group of students gathered around Gabe's seat in the back. Robin looked up and saw Jerry, whispered to the others, and they scattered back to their own seats, stifling laughs and stuffing photos into their notebooks.

Fortunately, no one said anything about the ice-skating incident, and Jerry thought maybe he'd be spared any real teasing. At least during first period.

But when Ms. Robertson began reviewing parts of speech, and she asked someone to make up a sentence with at least one prepositional phrase, Gabe raised his hand.

"You have a sentence, Gabe?" Ms. Robertson asked, surprised.

Gabe rarely volunteered anything worthwhile in

class. But Jerry figured he knew what Gabe was up to, and he braced himself.

"Yeah," Gabe said. "How about this? *The boy skated across the rink on shaking legs and crashed in a pathetic heap on the ice.*"

The classroom exploded in laughter.

Ms. Robertson appeared perplexed. "Well, that's certainly a sentence with a lot of prepositional phrases." She frowned at the back of the classroom. "Did I miss something?"

"Uh, you sort of had to be there, Ms. R.," Robin said, laughing.

"I'll tell you later, Zoey," Cinnamon called out. Zoey rolled her eyes.

Brenda scowled back at Gabe.

But Jerry sat still, his arms folded, looking straight ahead. This time, his face wasn't red. He even smiled a little at Brenda.

They could laugh all they wanted. He was feeling better and better, because in just a few hours, Gabe would pay.

"So, are you going to tell us now?" Brenda asked.

Kim and Kat Henley stood just behind Brenda, and all three were smiling expectantly.

Jerry had made them wait till after school to hear his plan. When the final bell rang, he hurried them to their lockers.

"In order for this to work, we have to move

quickly," he said. "Gabe always walks home through the park, right?"

"Yes," Brenda said. "With Craig. And sometimes Cinnamon tags along."

Jerry grinned. "Great. Let's go."

Jerry explained his plan to the girls on the way to the park.

"How are you going to get Gabe to go where you want him?" Kim asked.

"Oh, that's the easiest part," Jerry said, smiling. "I'm using myself for bait."

"I think it just might work," Brenda said.

"Me, too," Kat said, and Kim nodded.

It took five minutes to get set up, and they were all in their positions when Gabe, Craig, and Cinnamon came walking over the slope at the edge of the park.

Jerry sat alone under a tree. He pretended to concentrate on his science textbook.

He heard Gabe say "Flack" softly, and footsteps shuffled toward him. "Hey, Flack," Gabe called.

"Hi, Jerry," Cinnamon said.

Jerry looked up. "Hi."

Craig grinned. "That was some skating party, wasn't it, Flack?"

"Yeah," Jerry said. "It was."

Craig laughed. "You did some pretty fancy skating." He threw his arms out, imitating Jerry's gyrations on the ice.

"Now, Craig," Cinnamon said. "Be nice."

"Wanna see the pictures I took?" Gabe asked him. "Might as well. Everybody else in school has seen them."

"You're very photogenic, Flack," Craig said. "I especially liked the one where your mouth is hanging way open."

"Okay," Jerry said. "I'll look at them." He didn't move from his spot.

Gabe took off his book bag and pulled out a handful of photos from a zippered pouch. He walked over to Jerry and held them out.

Jerry snatched the pictures from Gabe, grabbed his book, and scrambled out of the way.

As a puzzled look crossed Gabe's face, some leaves rustled overhead, and from among the branches slid an enormous amount of gooey, green slime. It hit Gabe squarely on the top of his head and oozed over his shoulders and down the front of his shirt.

"What the—?" Gabe hollered. *"Yech!"* He hollered a few other words, too.

Brenda stepped out from behind some tall shrubs holding a camera. *Click click*, she snapped pictures.

Kim rushed out from behind another bush and handed Jerry a sword cut out of heavy cardboard.

"Back! Back, you evil slime monster!" Jerry hollered, brandishing his sword. "Don't worry, Cinnamon. I'll save you from this man-eating beast!"

The Henley sisters laughed while Brenda continued taking pictures, recording Jerry fighting off Gabe, whose front was nearly covered in the green slime.

Cinnamon was trying not to laugh, and Craig kept pacing around with a wild grin on his face, repeating, "Cool! Cool!"

"Flack!" Gabe screamed. "You better watch your back! I'm gonna get you for this!"

"You already did, Gabe," Brenda called out cheerfully, still snapping away. "This is *your* payback."

"Away with you, monster! Away!" Jerry, who had grown up reading comic books, was thoroughly enjoying this.

Gabe scooped a lot of the slime from his body with his hands, then rolled around on the grass to wipe off most of the rest. The gooey green stuff was still glommed in his hair, though. That wouldn't come out without a good shampoo under the shower, Jerry thought, feeling pleasantly satisfied.

Gabe grabbed up his book bag and pointed a finger in Jerry's face.

"You asked for it, Flack," he roared. "You haven't seen paybacks till you see what I'm going to do to you."

Jerry grinned and saluted. "You were a good sport, Gabe. Thanks for starring in my drama. You'll be able to watch yourself soon on my new website."

"Really?" Cinnamon cried. "Will I be in it, too?"

Jerry turned to Brenda, his official photographer, and he gestured dramatically for her to answer.

"Yes, you were a necessary part of the scene," Brenda said. "You'll be performing soon on computers everywhere."

"Cool!" Cinnamon squealed.

Gabe gave one final roar and stormed off through the park.

"Hey, Gabe! Wait up!" Cinnamon called. She and Craig followed him into the park.

Kat dropped out of the tree holding a large bucket, and they all thumped Jerry on the back.

"That was brilliant!" Brenda cried.

"Did you see his face?" Kim said, laughing.

"I loved dumping that glop all over him," Kat said. "That was definitely one of the most delicious moments of my life. What was that stuff, anyway?"

Jerry grinned. "It's a heated mixture of water, and polyvinyl alcohol, with a solution of borax, water, and green food coloring. It gets very thick and slimy. Wasn't it cool?"

"The coolest," Brenda said.

"Unbelievably cool," said Kim.

"Gabe got his comeuppance," Kat said. "He deserved it."

"Yes, he did," Jerry said. "I can't wait to develop the photos and get them online. I got the website up over the weekend. Now all I have to do is add these pictures."

"I can't wait till all the kids start seeing it," Brenda said. "They'll be able to go to the computer classroom or the media center at school if they don't have computers at home."

Jerry hadn't felt so good in weeks. He'd actually done it. He'd paid Gabe back for the humiliation he'd suffered at the ice-skating rink.

And soon—very soon—everyone at school would know all about it.

Chapter Seven

Jerry sat at the desk in his room. He picked up his favorite picture of Gabe covered in green slime. He'd gotten the film developed at the drugstore before coming home from the park. The photos had turned out so well, he'd decided to put three of them on his website.

Jerry studied the picture and grinned. Gabe really did look like a monster. His face, covered with green muck, was screwed up in a furious scowl. His mouth was wide open, roaring his anger at Jerry. Jerry stood bravely in profile, slashing at the monster with his sword. He looked as if he were defending Cinnamon, who stood at the edge of the picture, her eyes as big as saucers.

It was perfect.

Jerry lay the picture face down in his scanner. He hit the scan button, and the light tray underneath slid back and forth. He saved the picture as slimegabe1.jpg and exhaled with a satisfied sigh. Now all he had to do was scan the other pictures and put them on the website.

Voices from the yard drifted through his open window.

"You just climb the ladder to get into the tree house."

Jerry shifted in his chair and saw Cory and two other girls he didn't know scrambling up the ladder. Cory's friends were her size, probably third graders. He watched as they climbed into the tree house.

"Wow!" one of the girls said, looking out over the yard.

"What'd I tell ya? Isn't it cool?" Cory said.

"Whose tree house is this?" one of the girls asked.

"Well, it's Melissa Flack's yard," Cory said. "But she said I could play here anytime I wanted."

"Hey, Cory!" Melissa called from the back gate.

Jerry saw his sister cross the yard, and he nodded, glad she was home to supervise the girls in her tree house.

Jerry went back to his work. He was going to superimpose an arrow onto the photo that would point out Gabe, covered with slime. Next to the arrow, it would say, "Gabe Marshall, a.k.a. The

Green Slime Monster." And an arrow, pointing to Jerry would say, "Jerry Flack, hero monster-fighter. He'd appreciate your vote for sixth-grade president."

Jerry grinned; he was having a great time. He was glad Brenda had talked him into running. This practically even made up for the humiliation at the ice rink.

Jerry picked up the three pictures that Gabe had given him in the park. The pictures froze Jerry in three different humiliating poses: mid-totter, mid-fall, and sprawling on the ice. Jerry glanced at them, and scowled. His parents had a shredder in the den. That's what he'd do; he'd destroy them. He got up and headed out of his room. But he stopped in the middle of the hall.

Maybe he shouldn't destroy them, he thought. After all, the pictures had fueled his desire to get back at Gabe. What if he needed them again to inspire other acts of vengeance?

Jerry returned to his room and tossed the pictures into his bottom desk drawer. They'd be there if he needed them again.

"Hey, Melissa!" Cory's voice drifted into Jerry's room on the breeze. "You got some Cokes?"

"Sure," Melissa said. "I'll go get some."

"And hurry it up, will ya?" Cory said. "We're really thirsty. We need three."

"Okay."

What about four? Jerry thought. Wasn't Melissa

supposed to get a soda, too? After all, it was her yard and her tree house. And her Cokes.

Melissa wasn't the kind of kid who'd let anybody walk all over her, though, Jerry thought. She'd be okay.

He scanned the other two pictures. These were close-ups of Gabe. In one, Gabe was screaming at the camera, and in the other, he was rolling on the grass, trying to wipe off the slime. Jerry was sure that the kids at school would think they were funny. Especially because Gabe had passed around those pictures of Jerry flailing around on the ice. The kids would know that Jerry had scored a few points in his favor.

Jerry remembered Gabe's threat at the park. *"You haven't seen paybacks till you see what I'm going to do to you."* Jerry hadn't allowed himself to think about it very much—he didn't want to ruin his moment of victory. But Jerry knew that Gabe wasn't the sort of person who would take this lying down, especially after kids started seeing the funny—but embarrass-ing—pictures of him on Jerry's website.

Jerry would have to be very careful and watch his back, as Gabe had warned.

But, in the meantime, Jerry decided to allow himself to enjoy winning this particular battle.

Jerry couldn't wait to see Brenda's face when she saw his website. Without telling her where they were going, he dragged her down the hall toward the media center just before school. He saw Kim and Kat Henley and called out to them, "Follow us. I have a surprise."

"What's going on?" Kim asked.

"Yeah," Kat said. "This isn't like Jerry."

"He's not the mysterious type," Kim said.

"Except for yesterday," Kat said. "Remember, he wouldn't tell us his plan for getting back at Gabe till we were on our way to the park."

Brenda gasped. "Is it the website? Jerry, you have Gabe's pictures up *already*?"

"See for yourself," Jerry said, grinning. He steered her into the media center, guided her to a computer, and handed her a slip of paper. "Here's the address."

Brenda quickly typed in the address and, moments later, Jerry's home page appeared.

Jerry Flack for 6th Grade President

Jerry, in his school picture, smiled back at them. Along the side were buttons to click on. One said, "Jerry's Goals," and another said, "Jerry's Competition."

"I'll have more buttons in the next few days," Jerry explained. "I'll have one for Jerry's Qualifications and another one for Jerry's Top-Ten Favorite

Things About Hawthorne."

Brenda smiled and clicked to see the page on Jerry's competition.

When the image of a slimy, screaming Gabe came up on the monitor, Brenda shrieked with laughter.

"This is so great, Jerry!" she said. "He looks like such a— a—"

"A monster!" Kim said.

"A meanie," Kat said.

"A jerk," Kim said.

"Yeah, would you want this guy to be the president of your class?" Brenda asked. "I don't *think* so."

A couple of sixth-grade girls, one blonde and one dark haired, who were wandering by stopped to look over Brenda's shoulder. The blonde gasped and laughed, "Is that Gabe Marshall?"

Jerry grinned. "Yeah. I sort of slimed him in the park yesterday."

"What a riot!" she said.

"Oh, you're the guy he took pictures of at the ice rink," said the dark-haired girl. "Good for you!"

"Yeah, Gabe was really mean," the other girl said. She looked back at the monitor and grinned. "I can't believe that's good-looking Gabe Marshall."

"Oh, it's Gabe, all right," Brenda said.

"Wait till Wendy sees it," the first girl said. "She has such a crush on him. Maybe this'll cure her."

"Let's go get her. What's the address?"

Jerry wrote it down for her, and the girls hurried out of the media center, giggling.

"I wanted to get more stuff up on the site before anyone else saw it," Jerry said. "It's still under construction."

"I say, let 'em come and see it," Brenda said. "In the meantime, you can keep making the site better and better. The sooner the word gets out that your website is up, the sooner more kids will know about you and your campaign."

"And about how you got even with Gabe," Kat said.

"Yeah, that showed guts," Kim said.

Kat frowned at Jerry. "I have a question."

"What?"

"Aren't you afraid that Gabe'll decimate you?" Kat asked. "He sure was mad at the park yesterday."

"If you can dish out humiliation," Jerry said, "you'd better be ready to take it."

"I have a feeling that Gabe won't be philosophical on that point," Kat said. "He's just going to do something mean back to you."

"And then you'll have to retaliate," Kim said. "Again."

"Which will make him do some other nasty thing," Kat said.

"And you'll have to get even one more time," Kim said.

"It'll never end," Kat said.

"Until the election," Kim added.

"Maybe not even then," Kat said.

Kim turned to Jerry. "What if it goes on *forever*?"

Jerry stared at the twins. "I just want to enjoy this day, okay?" He glanced at Brenda. "If there's more trouble from Gabe, I'll deal with it then."

Brenda gazed at Jerry levelly. "In spite of their overzealousness, Flack, they do have a point," she said. "But I agree with you. For now, I think you should enjoy the moment."

Jerry turned his attention back to the picture of Gabe. "Yeah," he said, grinning. "One of the great things about having Gabe all slimed up like that on my website is that I can come back and enjoy the moment over and over, whenever I feel like it."

"And so can everyone else," Brenda said cheerfully.

Jerry sighed contentedly. "Score one for the Flackmeister," he said.

Chapter Eight

By lunchtime, the web address that Jerry had given the girls in the media center had made the rounds at school.

"Hey, Jerry, I saw the pictures of Gabe on your website," Aubrey Lane said in the hall outside the cafeteria. "It was hilarious!"

"Hey, Flack! Cool pictures of Marshall on the website!" Jonathan Peters hollered as Jerry entered the cafeteria.

Jane Baldus waved and smiled and gave Jerry a thumbs-up from the line where she stood waiting to get her lunch.

"We didn't even need to make a poster to advertise your website," Brenda said, grinning. "*Everybody* is running to the media center between classes to look it up. They all want to see Gabe with the green glop all over him. I guess Gabe hadn't heard about it before first hour. He didn't say anything in language arts class."

"I bet he's heard about it now," Kim said. "You're becoming something of a celebrity, Jerry." She and Kat had entered the line just behind Jerry and Brenda.

"I've noticed kids pointing you out to other kids," Kat said.

Jerry frowned. "Bren, you think I did the right thing?"

"Are you kidding?" Brenda said. "You paid Gabe back big time. He had it coming. Everyone says so."

"Everyone," Kim agreed, nodding.

"But maybe it wasn't the smart thing to do," Jerry said. "Maybe Kim and Kat are right. You heard what Gabe said at the park. He's going to get back at me."

Brenda shrugged. "If he does, you'll just play another trick on him."

Jerry sighed deeply. "I guess," he said. But he didn't feel ready to wage a two-person war. These skirmishes were enough. He hoped that Gabe would leave it alone now.

Jerry, Brenda, and the Henley sisters picked up their lunches in the line and headed for their table.

"Hey, Flack!" It was Craig Fox, sitting at a lunch

table with Gabe. "I saw the website." He dug an elbow into Gabe's side, and Gabe shoved him back, angrily. He laughed. "It was pretty cool. I'm showin' it to Gabe after lunch. But you better watch your back, Flack. He's real mad. And when Gabe gets mad, he does something about it, you know?"

"No, I don't know," Brenda said, her eyes narrow and her voice tight with anger. "Gabe deserved it for being so mean to Jerry at Skate Land. If he can't take humiliation, he should stop heaping it on other people."

"Bren," Jerry said softly. "Come on. Let's go."

Craig laughed again as Jerry guided Brenda to their table. The Henley sisters followed.

"I'm sorry, I couldn't help it," Brenda said, taking her seat at the long lunch table next to Chad and Tony. "Gabe's such a jerk."

"I was ready to give him a piece of my mind, too," Kim said. She plopped down next to her sister.

Kat rolled her eyes. "Riiight," she said.

"You don't think I would?" Kim asked her sister.

"No way," Kat said. "You've never in your life demonstrated a willingness to stand up to somebody scary." She picked up her peanut butter sandwich and took a bite.

"Oh, yeah?" Kim said. "What about that time in third grade when I pushed that fifth-grade bully into the mud?"

"You accidentally bumped into him and knocked

him over," Kat said around a mouthful of sandwich. "When you realized what you'd done, you ran for your life to Mrs. Belzer's. You rang her doorbell and told her you had to come in or a serial killer would make you his next victim."

"I didn't know what else to tell her," Kim said defensively.

"You could've just said you had to go to the bathroom or something," Kat said. "She would've let you in."

"Hey, guys—" Brenda said. They turned to her. "Cool it, will you? We should be reassuring Jerry."

"Yeah, Jerry," Chad said. "You did the right thing."

"I'm glad you gave Gabe a taste of his own medicine," Tony added.

Jerry pushed the food around his plate. He didn't have an appetite. "I think I'll skip lunch," he said.

He got up.

"Where are you going?" Brenda asked.

"For a walk," he said. He headed toward the cafeteria door.

"Can I have your goulash?" Kat called after him.

Jerry didn't feel like answering. He walked out of the cafeteria, turned left, and headed down the hall to the media center.

He strode to a study carrel on the far side of the large room. He wanted to be alone for a few minutes to think. He slipped behind the carrel, fitting himself into the chair between the carrel and the wall, like a sheet of paper into an envelope.

That was better. No one was here to bug or congratulate him about the website.

What bothered Jerry was having to battle with Gabe. Jerry wasn't a fighter. He didn't feel comfortable around conflict and physical threats. His family was pretty low-key, and having to "watch his back," as Gabe and Craig had put it, was completely beyond his experience. He just wanted to run a fun campaign in his bid for the sixth-grade presidency.

Footsteps lumbered over the carpet near Jerry's carrel.

"Wait till you see this, Marshall," Craig said, chortling. "You're gonna be real mad!" The footsteps stopped. Jerry figured the boys had paused at a computer table about fifteen feet from him, and he ducked lower behind the carrel.

He heard the soft tapping of computer keys.

"There it is," Craig's voice said. He laughed. "You look pretty funny, Marshall."

Jerry was suddenly overwhelmed with curiosity. How would Gabe take seeing himself covered in green glop? He raised himself up from his chair just enough to peek over the top of the carrel.

He saw Gabe's face, and it wasn't what Jerry had expected.

He thought Gabe would be furious. And he

thought he'd feel scared, looking at Gabe's angry face.

But Gabe didn't look mad, at least not at first. He looked mortified. He looked as embarrassed as Jerry had felt at the ice rink.

Gabe Marshall—the tough guy, the jock, the handsome kid that every girl had to look at twice—looked as if he might cry.

Jerry lowered himself back into his chair. He couldn't believe it, but he felt sorry for Gabe.

Maybe Gabe wasn't such a tough guy, after all. Maybe he had feelings, too.

Jerry slumped in the chair, feeling horrible. The only thing he had accomplished by humiliating Gabe was lowering himself to Gabe's level. And that was clearly at the bottom of Homo sapiens's development. He was as much of a jerk as Gabe.

Jerry waited until Gabe and Craig headed out of the library. Gabe was murmuring so softly that Jerry couldn't hear what he was saying.

Jerry sighed heavily. He got up and trudged out of the media center, knowing what he had to do as soon as he got home.

Chapter Nine

"You sure you want to take Gabe's pictures off your website?" Brenda asked. She shifted her book bag slightly to one side and crunched a leaf under her foot on the sidewalk. "And what's the hurry, anyway? We didn't need to skip the science team meeting. You could've shown everybody your cool volcano demonstration."

"I just want to take Gabe's pictures off my website before the whole school sees them," Jerry said. "Thanks for coming home with me. I guess I needed a reality check. I'm not crazy for wanting to get rid of his pictures, am I?" Brenda opened her mouth to answer, but Jerry kept walking, his head down, and continued, "You should have seen his face, Bren. I couldn't believe it was Gabe. He looked hurt and sad and alone."

Brenda frowned. "Just the way you looked at Skate Land."

"Exactly."

"Well, you can take his pictures off if you want to," Brenda said. "But it sure was getting you noticed at school. People who'd never heard of you before suddenly knew who you were. I'm sure it helped the campaign."

"I think they knew who I was because of the way I crashed and burned on the ice last Friday night," Jerry said. "A lot of the class was there. And the rest of them saw the pictures Gabe passed around."

"Well, I think you should do whatever makes you feel best," Brenda said. "The Henleys and Tony and Chad are coming over tonight to make posters. Did you notice some posters for secretary and treasurer up on the wall already? We need to get yours up, too. We'll list the things you want to do as president. We'll keep to the high road."

"Great," Jerry said. "Thanks. Gabe hasn't put up any posters yet."

Brenda smiled. "I'm glad you put Gabe's monster picture on your website, even if it was only for a day. It was fun to see him squirm."

Jerry grinned back. "It was fun, wasn't it? At least until I realized I wasn't any better than he was."

Brenda took his hand. "You're a classy guy, Jerry Flack."

Jerry liked the feel of Brenda's hand in his. It was cool and dry.

"I'm not so sure about that," he said. "If I were a classy guy, I wouldn't have paid Gabe back in the first place."

"A classy guy admits when he's made a mistake."

Jerry gazed at Brenda. What would he do without her? he wondered. He didn't say it out loud. She'd probably like to hear it. But he knew he'd turn fire-engine red if he ever uttered those words to her face.

They were about a block from his house when Jerry saw two little girls walking up the sidewalk. They were small, probably kindergartners, and they clutched large papers with crayon drawings that flapped in the breeze.

Just then, three bigger kids jumped out from behind a tall row of lilac bushes. Each wore a Halloween mask, and they let out monstrous roars like wild animals, their fingers splayed and bent like deadly lion claws.

The little girls screamed and took off running down the sidewalk. One of them let go of the picture she'd drawn, but she didn't even look back. She just cried and ran desperately to escape her attackers.

The three tormentors—one was smaller than the other two—took off their masks and hooted with laughter.

"Look at 'em run!" said one of the big girls.

"Yeah. Boy, were they scared!" said the smaller girl.

"Man," Brenda said. "Kids learn meanness when they're awfully young."

Jerry blinked and stared hard at the three girls. "I can't believe what I'm seeing," he said.

"What?"

"See the smaller girl?"

Brenda frowned into the distance. "*Melissa?* I can't believe it. What are you going to do?"

Jerry summoned up his most forceful voice. "*Melissa!*"

Melissa's head jerked around, and her smile faded. "Oh, hi, Jerry," she said in tiny mouse-like tones.

"Come here," he said.

"Oh, spit," Melissa muttered. She glanced self-consciously at Cory and the other girl. "I'll see you guys later."

"We'll meet you at the tree house," Cory piped up.

Cory and her friend ran down the sidewalk toward the Flacks' house.

"Don't be too hard on her," Brenda whispered before Melissa was close enough to hear. "She was trying to fit in with the big kids."

Melissa stopped in front of Jerry, a look of defiance on her face.

"What do you want?" she said.

"I've never seen you do anything mean like

that," Jerry said. "Why would you want to scare those little kids?"

Melissa stared at the ground and didn't speak.

Jerry wasn't in the habit of disciplining his sister, and he felt weird. But he couldn't ignore how cruel she'd been to those kids.

So he said, "Remember that time when you were about four and we went to Aunt Margaret's house? And her son Dirk kicked your stack of blocks all over the room and scared you to death? You cried for an hour."

Melissa shrugged.

"I know you remember how awful it was to be scared by a bully." Melissa didn't respond, and Jerry decided to change the subject. "You, uh, want to see a science trick when we get home?"

"No. I'm playing with Cory and Amber." She continued to stare at the sidewalk.

"Okay," Jerry said. "Suit yourself."

Melissa looked up now, the same defiance in her eyes. "You gonna tell Mom?"

"No, I'm not going to tell Mom."

Melissa's eyes narrowed. "Dad?"

"Nope."

Melissa looked confused, then straightened her shoulders. "So can I go now?"

"Yes," Jerry said. "But I have to tell you, Missy, you surprised me today."

Melissa rolled her eyes. "Get over it, Jerry." She

turned and ran down the sidewalk toward home.

Jerry blinked at Brenda, his eyes wide. "'Get over it, Jerry'?"

Brenda grinned and shook her head. "First graders. You gotta love 'em."

"Who says so?" Jerry muttered.

"Jerry! Did you look out the front window?"

Jerry opened his eyes and squinted up at his mother and father. He glanced at the clock on his bedside table, which read 6 A.M.

"The front window?" Jerry asked, blinking. "No, I'm asleep." He didn't point out that his clock was set for 6:15 every morning, and that he was *supposed* to have another fifteen minutes in dreamland before having to get up for school.

"Just *look* at what they did to our trees!" his mother said. "You're going to have to get up right now and go outside and clean up as much as you can reach with a rake."

"It's quite a mess," his dad said, nodding. "I hope it doesn't rain today."

Jerry frowned and hauled himself up to a sitting position. He swung his legs to the floor, got up, and walked into his parents' room. He looked out the front window.

Without his glasses, it looked as though the two maples in the front yard were covered with white, fluffy blossoms. But, of course, he knew that maples are not flowering trees that bloom in the fall. There was only one way that the trees could turn white overnight.

Toilet paper.

It clung to nearly every twig. He'd never seen so much TP on one tree in his life. Whoever did it was an expert.

"Wow," he said. *"Cool."*

"Cool?" his mother said from behind him. "Are you kidding?"

Jerry's dad guided his mother out of the bedroom. "Let's let Jerry handle it," he murmured.

Jerry got dressed, all the while thinking. He really *was* getting noticed! Nobodies were ignored. You had to be a *somebody* to get your trees TPed.

He slipped his camera into his pocket, and once he was outside, he took several shots. Brenda would never believe the extent of the papering without seeing graphic proof of the scene.

Jerry wondered if Gabe was behind this. Probably. Jerry smiled. If Gabe used this to get back at him for putting the monster picture on the website, Jerry was happy. This wasn't bad. In fact, it was quite flattering. The neighbors would know that somebody *important* lived here.

He whistled to himself as he walked to the garage to get the rake and a garbage can.

Chapter Ten

"Hey, Jer." Craig Fox leaned against the locker next to theirs, a devilish grin on his face. "Notice anything in your front yard this morning?"

Jerry turned to him and frowned. "What do you mean?"

Craig looked surprised. "I mean, didn't you see anything—unusual outside?"

Jerry shrugged and willed himself not to smile. "No. What are you talking about?"

"Uh, nothing." Craig's eyes glazed over in confusion. "So what's your address?"

"Why?"

"Nothing. Never mind." Craig hurried away. Jerry took out the books he needed for the morning and closed his locker. Now he allowed himself a smile. He figured Craig and Gabe would frantically look up his address in the phone book this morning, wondering if they'd hit the wrong house.

"Hi, Flack. What's funny?" Brenda asked.

"Wait till you see the pictures of the TP job Gabe did on my house. It was awesome!" Jerry and Brenda headed down the hall to language arts class. "Mom and Dad weren't too happy about it, though."

"What a shock," Brenda said. "May I guess who was pulled out of bed this morning to clean it up?"

"It'll take *days* to clean up all that paper," Jerry said and added with a note of respect, "It was very thorough, very professional."

"Remind me to congratulate Gabe on a job well done."

"No, don't say anything. I pretended to Craig that I hadn't noticed it." Jerry laughed. "Drove him crazy."

"I'll bet," Brenda said. "What's the fun of pulling a trick on somebody if they don't react?"

"Right," Jerry said. "That's the whole idea."

"Hey, we made some great posters for you last night," Brenda said. "We'll show you at lunch and put them up between classes this afternoon."

"Thanks, Bren."

Brenda smiled. "I'm getting into this, Flack," she said. "And I can say, 'I helped make Jerry Flack the best sixth-grade president that Hawthorne Middle School ever had.'"

Jerry smiled back. That sounded good to him.

Jerry's PE class was sixth period, the second to the last in the day. As usual, he went to the locker room, where he dressed in the shorts and T-shirt he'd brought from home at the beginning of the school year. He left his regular school clothes in his locker, a wire basket that padlocked to a steel loop on the basket shelf.

Jerry didn't like PE, especially when they played basketball or worked out with the gymnastic equipment. But they were going to play kickball today, so he figured it wouldn't be too bad. If you can kick the ball hard enough, Jerry thought, it didn't matter if you couldn't run particularly fast. And Jerry had a very strong kicking leg.

Walking with the other kids out to the softball diamond, Jerry glanced back and thought he saw Gabe slip in the back door to the locker rooms. But that was impossible, Jerry thought. He knew for sure that Gabe had science this period—he was in Jeff Gnagy's class. One time, Jeff had mentioned what a bonehead Gabe was about science. So it must have been someone wearing a shirt like Gabe's. Besides, what possible reason would Gabe have for being in the gym area during science period? Jerry shook his head and didn't give it another thought.

Jerry scored two points for his kickball team that afternoon, so he was feeling pretty good when the class was over. He received a bunch of high fives on the way to the locker room. Inside, he went to his locker basket, which he found without a lock and empty.

Jerry stared at the locker. "Wha—? Where are my clothes?" he murmured.

"What's the matter?" Brad Hackbarth asked. Brad spun the dial on his combination lock, right next to Jerry's locker.

"My clothes are gone," Jerry said. "I locked my locker. How could it be open?"

"You sure you put your stuff in *that* locker?" Brad asked.

"Of course, I'm sure," Jerry said. "This is my locker." Brad frowned. "I had the combination lock on it, the one I brought from home. Even the lock is gone."

"Maybe someone cut if off," Brad observed.

"Somebody cut off your lock?" Nick Fenneman asked. He was using the locker on Jerry's other side.

Three more guys gathered around. Then four, then five.

"Yeah," Jerry said, absentmindedly scratching his neck. It didn't take much heavy thinking to figure out who was responsible for his missing clothes.

It *was* Gabe he'd seen sneaking into the locker room just after class started. He'd skipped out on science so he could break, enter, and steal. He must have used heavy-duty metal cutters to get through the lock. Or—

Jerry wheeled around and saw Craig Fox watching him, his eyes bright and a half smile on his face. Craig smiled a little more, threw a T-shirt over his head, and turned away.

Craig could have watched over Jerry's shoulder to learn his locker combination. He could have told Gabe, who then sneaked in and stole his clothes.

"You have any idea who did it?" Nick asked.

"No," Jerry said.

"Hey, what about Gabe Marshall?" Brad suggested. "He's running against you for president, right? He took those pictures of you at Skate Land? And didn't you pour green muck all over him at the park?"

"Uh, yeah," Jerry said.

"I bet it was Marshall," Nick said, grinning. "You going to get him for this?"

"I don't know for sure it was Gabe," Jerry said.

"Five bucks says it was Marshall," Brad said.

"Yeah, it was Marshall, all right," Nick agreed.

Jerry's mind shifted to his immediate problem. What was he going to do? His parents were both teaching today at the university, so no one was home to drive a change of clothes to school. Besides, his mother was likely to go berserk. *("I paid good money for those clothes!"* and *"How could anyone be so mean?"* and *"I'm going to get to the bottom of this."*) She'd head directly to the principal and make a federal case out of it. Jerry didn't want his mother to get involved.

"You gonna tell Mr. Gunther?" Nick asked.

"No," Jerry said. He had no doubt that Gabe was behind this—and Craig at least knew about it—but he had no proof. And what would telling the gym teacher accomplish, anyway? What if Gabe were given a suspension? Would that make him stop doing mean things to Jerry? Not likely.

"What're you gonna do?" Brad asked. "Wear your gym clothes for seventh period?"

"I guess it's the only thing I *can* do," Jerry said. "I don't have any other clothes."

Brad and Nick and the rest of the guys laughed. "Hey, I'm glad I don't have seventh hour with you," Brad said. "'Cause those gym clothes reek, Flack."

Jerry winced. He'd been smelling them all period. "Yeah," he said. "I know. I know."

Jerry walked down the hall toward his computer class, which was the last period of the day. If the weather had been hot lately, he wouldn't have felt self-conscious, because the other students would be wearing shorts, too.

But the weather had cooled off during the last few days, and the temperature hadn't reached higher than 50 degrees. So Jerry was the only student in shorts and a T-shirt. Students walking by in sweatshirts glanced at him as he made his way down the hallway. Some of them smiled, but nobody said anything.

Until he was passing Gabe and Craig on the second floor.

"Nice legs, Flack," Gabe said, smirking.

Craig slapped Jerry on the back. "Flack," he said, "those are the skinniest legs I've ever seen."

Jerry forced a smile. "And thanks to you guys, I get to show them off," he said cheerfully.

Several students who heard the exchange laughed and looked at Jerry's skinny, white legs and his knobby knees.

From the corner of his eye, Jerry saw a flash and turned back down the hall. Gabe had just taken a picture of him. Gabe laughed and cried, "Oh, man!" then turned and headed away.

Jerry walked toward class. Even though he didn't like it that Gabe had taken a picture of him, he felt glad that he hadn't shown Gabe and Craig how rattled he was about losing his clothes. Jerry was also glad that with his "thanks to you guys" comment, he'd made it clear that he knew who broke into his gym locker.

Now students on either side of him looked and laughed and pointed. Jerry smiled and nodded at them.

The laughter grew.

"Look at that," someone said, sneering. "He doesn't even know."

What was going on? Doesn't know what? Jerry knew his legs were ugly, but they didn't deserve this much attention.

"Hey, Flack!" someone yelled. "I wouldn't vote for those legs if they were the last legs on earth!"

"What?" Jerry asked.

Chad Newsome hurried up behind him, and Jerry felt a tug at his shirt.

"Someone put a sign on your back," Chad said and handed him the notebook paper with a piece of tape on it.

Would you vote for these skinny legs for president?

Jerry grabbed the paper and crumpled it while kids laughed all around him.

"What a sap," one guy said, shaking his head.

"I wonder how long he was walking around like that?" another guy said, laughing.

"What a dork," a girl chortled.

Jerry felt his face heat up. "Thanks, Chad," he said in a low voice.

"No problem." Chad looked down at Jerry's clothes. "What's going on?"

"A minor problem in gym class. Gabe stole my

clothes." Jerry hung his head and held up the crumpled paper. "Then Craig slapped this on my back."

"Sorry, man," Chad said.

"Yeah."

Jerry turned in to his computer class.

Brenda had already arrived. She sat in her usual seat next to Jerry's. She frowned when she saw him.

"What's with the shorts, Flack?" she asked, examining him. "Aren't those your PE clothes?" The odor apparently wafted her way, and she wrinkled her nose and coughed. "Yup, those are your PE clothes."

Jerry sank into his seat, miserable.

"What happened?" Brenda asked. "You okay?"

"Don't ask." Jerry tried to muster up some anger to replace the humiliation. He cleared his throat. "Gabe stole my clothes out of my gym locker."

"What!" Brenda cried. She sat back in her seat and leveled a gaze at Jerry. "And you felt sorry for him and took his pictures off your website."

"Then he and Craig stuck a sign on my back." Jerry tossed the crumpled paper to Brenda, who spread it out on her desk.

"Oh! This is just like Gabe. He's such a jerk, such a creep, such a—" She stopped. "Don't you want to get him back? I'd like to push his face in!"

"Thanks, Bren," Jerry said. "But this just confirms what I said about Gabe. I don't want to operate at his level. Not anymore."

Brenda blew out a breath. "Gabe is keeping his promise about getting back at you, all right."

"I hope this is the end of it," Jerry said. "Maybe if I don't react, he'll stop."

"Well, I wouldn't count on it."

Sara Neville walked past, wearing a sweatshirt over a turtleneck, and she frowned. "Aren't you cold, Jerry? How come you're wearing shorts?"

Jerry forced a smile. "I like to test myself," he said cheerfully. "I see how much discomfort I can stand. I want to be an astronaut some day."

"Your legs are covered in goose bumps."

Jerry smiled. "I can take it."

She shrugged and took her seat in the back of the room.

Brenda leaned over. "Well, Flack, I hope you *can* take it. We know that Gabe is a total jerk, and he's not likely to have a personality transplant anytime soon."

Jerry sighed. Brenda was right. It would be just like Gabe to cook up more humiliation for him.

He wondered how much more he could stand.

Chapter Eleven

"Come here, Sassy." Jerry called her from the back door. She lay in the grass under the tree house, watching the activity above with longing in her eyes. "Come on, girl. You can't join in the fun up there."

Sassy got up and trotted to Jerry, her tail swinging. Jerry let her in the door and turned back toward the tree house.

"Melissa," Jerry called. "Mom says it's time to come in and wash your hands. We'll be having supper soon."

"Oh, spit!" Melissa said, stomping her foot on the tree house floor.

"Tell him okay, but don't go in till you get called

again," Cory said, her voice soft. She was hidden behind leafy branches, but her voice was unmistakable.

"Okay!" Melissa yelled to Jerry.

Jerry had an idea. He walked out into the yard and stopped under the tree. "You girls want to see a science trick?" he asked.

"Yuck, no," Melissa said, and an appreciative laugh followed from inside the tree house.

"Tell him to leave us alone," Cory murmured.

"Leave us alone, Jerry," Melissa said.

More snickers. Melissa's head disappeared behind the wall of the tree house.

After the day Jerry had had, he wasn't in any mood to let his little sister push him around. He was about to go up and drag her out of the tree house, but then he heard Cory's voice, speaking low.

"Okay, so take this note to Angie in my class," Cory said. "It'll make her real mad, but I hate her."

"Why don't you take it to her, yourself?" Melissa whispered back.

"'Cause *you're* gonna take it," Cory told her.

"How come?" Melissa asked. "I don't want to give it to her if it'll make her mad." She added defiantly, "I'm not your slave, y'know."

"Okay," Cory said. Then she added with a dark edge to her voice, "But if you don't take it to her, I won't be your friend anymore."

Blackmail, Jerry thought. Melissa's playing with a third-grade blackmailer.

He wanted to tell Cory to go home and leave Melissa alone. But he knew that wouldn't solve the problem. Melissa looked up to Cory and obviously wanted to play with her.

Jerry walked back to the house. He'd have to let this work itself out, he thought. Melissa wasn't interested in hearing what he had to say about anything. She was taking her orders from a younger authority these days.

Jerry walked along the upstairs hall that evening and passed Melissa's room. She sat on her bed, staring at a piece of folded paper in her hand.

Jerry paused in the doorway.

"Hey, Missy," he said.

Melissa's head jerked up, and she shoved the paper under a pair of jeans lying across the bed. "Yeah?" she said, scowling. "What do you want?"

Jerry shrugged. "Just wondered what you're doing."

"Nothing." She stared at Jerry, her face blank.

Jerry frowned. He wanted to help Melissa but didn't know how to reach her. "You okay, Missy?"

Melissa flopped back on her bed with a loud sigh. "Yeah. Why?"

"Just wondered," he said.

Melissa rolled over and hid her face in her pillow.

"You having fun in the tree house?"

"Yeah," she said. Her voice was muffled from the pillow, but Jerry didn't hear any joy in it.

"You haven't looked too happy lately."

Melissa rolled over to face him. "Sometimes I think I'm really stupid."

Jerry walked into her room, turned around the chair at her small desk, and straddled it. "I thought you were the smartest girl in your class."

Melissa shrugged. "I'm smart for a first grader, I guess." She thought a moment. "I wish I was in third grade. Or fourth. And bigger."

"Just because you're small, you don't have to let someone bigger push you around, you know," Jerry said.

Melissa answered in a small voice, "Yeah."

"You haven't played with Rachel lately," Jerry said. "Why don't you invite her over sometime?"

Melissa scratched her cheek. "I don't know. Rachel's not much fun," she said seriously. "She likes little-kid things. She's kind of immature, you know."

Yeah, she hasn't learned how to blackmail people yet, Jerry thought.

"She still plays with dolls," Melissa added, as if that would prove her point.

"Oh." Jerry got up. "Well, Missy, I bet you and Rachel would have a lot of fun in the tree house together."

"Maybe," Melissa said. Jerry turned to leave. "Jerry?"

"Yeah?"

"What would you do if someone told you to—" Her voice trailed off.

"Told you to what?"

A short silence filled the room. "Nothing," she said. She turned her head toward the wall again, signaling an end to the conversation.

"Hey, Flack," Craig said as he opened their locker the next morning. "You see the picture Gabe got developed last night?"

Jerry's heart lunged. *The picture Gabe took of him wearing the sign on his back.*

Jerry shrugged and turned away, pretending he was looking for something inside the locker. "Nope," he said.

Craig laughed. "It's a pretty funny picture, man. You got really scrawny legs, you know that? Gabe got lots of copies made, and he's passing them around. I'm sure you'll see one of 'em today."

"Great," Jerry said, hoping he sounded neutral about the prospect of seeing the embarrassing picture.

Jerry wished he could crawl into his locker and spend the day there. Or go home and read his science magazines. He wished he could do anything but stay here at school while kids were passing around the pictures and laughing at him.

And he hated feeling like such a coward. Why

couldn't he face a little teasing? He'd certainly been teased before, in his old school.

But that had been a tease in the hall, a small embarrassment on the sidewalk. This was so *public*. Gabe was making sure everyone knew about the tricks he pulled to make Jerry look stupid and dorky.

Jerry briefly considered coming up with another payback for Gabe, but he dismissed the thought right away. As embarrassed as he was being the brunt of Gabe's practical jokes, he didn't want to be the kind of guy who could humiliate another person and be proud of himself. Even if the person he humiliated was his worst enemy.

Jerry Flack was better than that.

At least, he hoped so.

Jerry first saw the picture in language arts. Gabe walked past him and dropped it on his desk. "Thought you might like a copy," Gabe said, sneering. "I have lots more."

Several of the students laughed.

Brenda swiveled in her seat to look at the photo of Jerry.

"Oh, no," Jerry murmured. It was worse than he had imagined.

In the photo, Jerry walked down the hall, his legs looking ghostly white and spindly as golf clubs. He was looking back over his shoulder toward the camera, his mouth hanging open, saying something.

The sign was stuck to the middle of his back. All the kids surrounding him were laughing and pointing at the sign.

Brenda seethed with anger. "I hate Gabe Marshall," she said. "I hate him so much, I could just—"

Jerry looked up at her. "You could just what?"

"I could just knock his head off."

Jerry nodded. "Not too practical, but thanks for the thought." He stared at the picture again, then glanced around to see if anyone was listening. He lowered his voice. "This is embarrassing, Bren. I look like such a—" He couldn't say it.

"You're going to say dork," Brenda said.

"Exactly."

"Well," Brenda said, "I don't think this will hurt your chances for becoming president. Gabe's just being mean."

Jerry nodded. "I wasn't even thinking about the campaign. This has gotten so—personal. Bren, will you collect as many of these pictures as you can? At least we can take some of them out of circulation."

"Yeah."

"Hey," Gabe called out to everyone in the class. "Did you guys see the picture of Flack I took yesterday?"

Jerry's stomach tensed. Around the room, heads turned and several students got up to look at the pictures Gabe spread out on his desk.

"Ha!" Scott Perkins said. "I heard about this picture, but it's even funnier than I thought it would be."

Other students gathered around Gabe's desk and laughed.

Just then, Cinnamon rushed into the room, an open magazine in her hands.

"You guys!" she called out. "This is so *cool*!"

Ms. Robertson entered the classroom as the bell rang. "Everyone take your seats," she said.

"Ms. R.!" Cinnamon said. "Guess who's in the new *People* magazine?"

"Should I be able to guess, Cinnamon?" Ms. Robertson asked, smiling.

"It's *Zoey*!" Cinnamon cried.

Zoey, who was at the back of the room, lifted her chin, frowning. "What are you talking about?"

Cinnamon stood at the front of the class beaming, basking in the glow of the sudden limelight.

"Listen to this, you guys." She cleared her throat. "There's this interview with that hot new actor, Josh McClellen? The *People* interviewer asked him, 'What do you like to do for a good time?' And this is his answer: 'My favorite time was going to parties at my friend Zoey's house. But she moved and disappeared off the face of the earth. I guess I'll have to find another girl to party with.'"

Cinnamon clutched the magazine to her chest and gazed with reverence at Zoey, slumped in the back of the room. "He's talking about you, isn't he?"

Zoey's face was serious. "Yeah. Josh was my bud."

"Wow. Cool," Robin said.

"Awesome," Gabe mumbled.

Everyone turned to look at Zoey.

"I can't believe Zoey's here at Hawthorne Middle School," Cinnamon said solemnly.

"Neither can I," Zoey muttered.

Jerry was glad the attention had shifted to Zoey. Maybe people would start talking about her and how she was mentioned in *People*, instead of that horrible picture that Gabe was passing around. After all, knowing a girl who parties with movie stars is a whole lot more interesting than looking at gross pictures of a white-legged sixth-grade boy.

"What luck," Jerry said at lunch. "That *People* magazine came out at exactly the right time. It's all everyone's talking about."

"But have you noticed?" Brenda said. "The kids aren't just talking about Zoey, they're *imitating* her. Look!" She pointed to the kids in the lunch line. Most of them were slouched over, looking bored out of their minds. "And there." She gestured to the table with Cinnamon and Robin and their girl friends. They were all drooping over their lunch, elbows on the table, propping up their heads in their hands. "And there." She waved her hand at kids in a group by the cafeteria entrance who were watching Zoey slumped at her lunch table. Several leaned against the wall, others rolled their eyes and sighed heavily.

"Amazing," Kat said. "Sixth graders are sheep."

"Yeah," Tony said. "They all follow the coolest sheep in the school."

"You think if Zoey Long jumped off a cliff, the rest of them would follow her?" Kim asked.

"It would be an interesting experiment," Chad offered, smiling.

"But we'd never convince Zoey to jump off the cliff in the first place," Kat said.

"Yeah. Some people just don't appreciate scientific research," Kim said.

The sisters burst into hysterical laughter.

"But it's not only sixth graders," Brenda said after their laughter had died down. "That *People* article has been photocopied and passed around to the seventh and eighth graders. They're slumping and drooping, too."

"Wow." Jerry had a hard time believing that one person could have so much power over other people. Then he remembered that just a few weeks ago, he was pretending he was a cool guy just to impress Cinnamon O'Brien. And his sister wasn't acting like herself these days so she could impress her third-grade friend Cory.

Maybe it wasn't so amazing, after all.

"It's an interesting phenomenon," Jerry observed. Then he grinned. "And I'm glad we saw it demonstrated here on *this* particular day."

"Yes, indeedy!" Brenda said. She laughed and gave him a high five. "And here are five of the pictures that Gabe took. Five fewer to get shown around school."

"Thanks," Jerry said. He slid them into his pocket. They'd go into his drawer at home with the others.

Kat spoke up. "I wonder if Gabe will think up another trick to play on Jerry, because this last one didn't have the effect he wanted."

Jerry's smile faded.

"Kat!" Brenda cried.

"Yeah, we're supposed to help Jerry feel better," Kim said.

"Sorry," Kat said.

Jerry sighed. Maybe Kat was right. They still had a week and a day left in the campaign. Maybe Gabe would need another trick to carry him through the week, something to propel him into office while the kids were laughing at Jerry.

Jerry made a mental note never to run for a real political office. He was realizing that there was a whole lot more to campaigning than debating the issues. If personal attacks, ridicule, and public humiliation were a part of running for office, Jerry didn't need to run another campaign. He'd had enough of that to last a lifetime.

Chapter Twelve

"We'll make this a quick trip," Jerry's mom said, pulling into a parking space at the Green Valley Mall.

Jerry hated shopping of any kind, and he usually only came to the mall when he was forced by one of his parents. But this time, he was here to get some clear plastic sleeves to hold name badges. He planned to make some I'm Voting for Jerry for President! pins. He would use a computer software program to create colorful badges with a cool design that would capture kids' attention in the halls at school.

"Why do I have to be here?" Melissa whined from the back seat. "I could stay home alone. Sassy could protect me."

The thought that their mischievous but sweet family dog would chase away burglars made Jerry laugh. "Yeah, Sassy could knock down an intruder and lick him into submission before the police arrived. Or maybe she'd get scared and hide under the bed."

"Shut up, Jerry," Melissa said.

"Melissa!" Jerry's mother turned to the back seat. "You know we don't say that in our family. And I had to bring you tonight. I can't buy you shoes without having your feet with me."

"You could've cut off her feet and brought them along without the rest of her," Jerry said helpfully.

"Shut up, Jerry."

"Stop that, Melissa!" Jerry's mother said, clearly exasperated. "Let's get what we need and go home." She got out of the car and shut the door.

"I can say whatever I want," Melissa mumbled.

"She can't hear you," Jerry said.

"Well, duh. You think I don't know that?"

Jerry rolled his eyes. "You've really been a pain lately, you know that? Come on. Let's go."

Jerry and Melissa climbed out of the car and followed their mother into the mall.

"Melissa and I will get the shoes upstairs," Jerry's mother said. "And you get what you need. We'll meet you at the fountain in the middle courtyard in"—she checked her watch—"a half hour."

"Okay."

Jerry headed down the mall corridor toward the drugstore. A familiar green jacket up ahead caught his eye.

Cinnamon, who was in the green jacket, stood stiffly next to Robin. Both girls looked worried.

"Hey," Jerry said, approaching.

"Oh, Jerry, you've got to do something!" Cinnamon said, waving her hands wildly. "Gabe's going to do like a tightrope walk on the railing of the second floor."

Jerry frowned. "Why would he do something—" He stopped short before adding "that stupid."

Cinnamon scowled. "To impress Zoey."

"Zoey?"

"He's trying to impress her," she said again, and added darkly, "and maybe he wants more than that." Cinnamon pointed. "She's over there. By the water fountain."

Zoey, who leaned against the wall, gazed with a bored expression at the corridor overhead.

Jerry followed her gaze. Gabe and Craig stood next to the railing on the second floor that overlooked the atrium. Both were grinning.

Gabe shoved a foot between the vertical bars on the railing and hoisted himself up so that the top of the railing was at his waist. Craig laughed.

"Cinnamon," Jerry said, "tell him to get down."

Cinnamon's eyes got big. "You mean, yell? In front of Zoey?"

"Of course!"

Cinnamon frowned. "Why don't *you* yell?"

Jerry rolled his eyes. "Because Gabe doesn't *listen* to me."

"Oh." Cinnamon stepped forward. "Gabe," she called out. "Stop it." She didn't sound at all convincing. "Come down here."

Gabe continued to grin and threw a leg over the railing.

"Cool!" Craig clapped and hooted with laughter.

A group of shoppers was gathering. A murmur of concern ran through the crowd.

Jerry ran over to Zoey. "Zoey, he's doing this to impress you. Tell him to get down."

Zoey stared up at Gabe, her face expressionless. "What an idiot," she said blandly.

"Tell him to get down!" Jerry cried. "He's going to kill himself if he falls!"

Zoey stared at Jerry. "And that would be bad because . . . ?" Her voice trailed off.

"Zoey!" Jerry couldn't believe her casual attitude.

Gabe yelled down. "Hey, Zoey! If I walk on this rail, you'll tell everyone you're voting for me, right?" He grinned idiotically.

"He's got to be kidding," Zoey muttered.

"He's not kidding, Zoey!" Jerry hollered in her face. "Tell him *no*, you won't support him."

"He won't do it," Zoey said.

"Get the security guard," a man called from the crowd.

"Tell Jerry to stay out of this," Gabe yelled, scowling. "What are you doing here, anyway, Flack?"

Jerry put his hands on his hips. "This is a mall, Gabe," he called out. "I'm *shopping*."

Gabe ignored him. "Will you vote for me if I walk on the rail, Zoey?"

"Tell him no!" Jerry cried at Zoey.

Zoey turned a level stare at Jerry. "I don't yell, Jerry," she said matter-of-factly.

"What's the problem with *yelling*?" Jerry cried. Zoey stared at him. "Then shake your head, okay? Can you do that? Just shake your head!"

Zoey shrugged then shook her head no at Gabe.

Just then, a security guard took Gabe firmly by the arm and made him crawl down off the railing.

"See?" Zoey said mildly. "A waste of a perfectly good head shake. He wouldn't have done it, anyway."

Jerry gawked at her and said sarcastically, "Well, thanks for all your trouble."

Zoey gazed at him steadily. "After all the stuff he's pulled on you, you wanted to stop him from doing something dangerous?"

"I don't like Gabe," Jerry said. "But I don't want to win the election just because he happens to die."

Zoey's eyebrows lifted. "Hmm." She seemed to think that over. "Okay. That's cool."

Jerry rolled his eyes. "See you," he said.

He hurried to the drugstore to get what he needed to make the campaign pins.

"So Gabe was really going to balance on that skinny rail, just to get Zoey's vote?" Brenda asked at lunch the next day.

"It sure looked like he was going to try," Jerry said. "But Zoey didn't believe him."

Kim's hand, holding a carrot stick, paused in mid-air before moving to her mouth. "Yet another demonstration of his immaturity," she said.

"Jerry," Brenda said, "you know the voting for class officers is a week from tomorrow. Have you thought about your campaign speech?"

Jerry's stomach flipped over. "Uh, no."

"We need to get busy on that," Brenda said. "You want me to come over this weekend, and we'll brainstorm?"

"Sure."

"We should do something really special to get the kids' attention," Brenda said.

"Like what?" Jerry asked. The very idea of speaking in front of the whole sixth grade sent adrenaline surging through his veins.

"I don't know," Brenda said. "Think about it, and we'll talk Saturday."

Jerry thought about the things that had happened

since he announced he'd run for president: Gabe had humiliated him at Skate Land; he'd lowered himself to Gabe's level in order to slime and embarrass him; his house had been TPed; Gabe had stolen his clothes and stuck a sign on his back. And Gabe had taken lots of embarrassing pictures of him and passed them around school.

None of these things had anything to do with what the campaign was supposed to be about: improving the sixth grade at Hawthorne Middle School. Some of the posters that Brenda and the Henley sisters had put up around the halls listed Jerry's website address and the things that Jerry wanted to do if he were elected president.

But nobody was talking about those things. All they seemed interested in were the very public tricks that Jerry and Gabe had played on each other.

It was time to take the campaign to a new, higher level, Jerry thought.

Brenda said, "We're going to win this election, Flack. I can feel it in my bones."

Jerry wished his bones could agree. Mostly, though, they just trembled at the thought of getting up in front of the entire sixth grade.

And Jerry had to wonder. If Gabe were willing to pull mean tricks on him, and risk his life to get Zoey's support for his campaign, winning must be pretty important to him.

What else was Gabe willing to do to get elected president?

"I have to go to the dentist's office," Brenda said after school. "Mom's picking me up. You want a ride? We'll be driving within a few blocks of your house."

"No, thanks," Jerry said. "Mr. Hooten's letting me borrow some science magazines over the weekend. I'm going to stop by his room before I leave."

"Okay, I'll see you Saturday to talk about your speech. Want to say about two o'clock?"

"Sounds good. The two o'clock, I mean. Not the speech."

Brenda laughed. "See you."

Jerry headed down the hall, which was already emptying of students eager to start their weekend.

"Psst!" Jerry glanced down a nearly empty, dead-end hall. Craig stood in the doorway of one of the two classrooms.

"Flack! Come here!" It came out as a stage whisper, one you could hear halfway down the corridor.

Jerry frowned. "Why? I have to go to the science room."

"Come on!"

Jerry sighed and walked toward Craig. The classroom behind him was dark. As he approached him, Jerry saw that no one was there.

Except Gabe.

Jerry stopped just outside the doorway. "What do you want?" he asked.

"So suspicious!" Gabe said. "Don't you think Jerry has a suspicious nature, Fox?"

"Yeah," Craig said. "Real suspicious."

The boys rushed at Jerry, grabbed him, and hauled him into the room. Gabe kicked the door closed behind him.

"What do you want?" Jerry cried, struggling to free his arms.

Gabe was very strong, and with Craig helping him, he didn't have any trouble dragging Jerry across the room and over to the window.

That's when Jerry realized that the window was *open*. Two stories down were dozens of students waiting to get onto school buses.

Gabe's and Craig's grip tightened on him.

"What are you doing?" Jerry asked, alarm spreading through his body. He fought harder.

"Get ready for another photo op," Gabe said. "Cinnamon's down below with a camera."

He and Craig lifted Jerry and shoved him head-first out the window while Jerry struggled ferociously. The ground wobbled below him where a mob of kids stood, their faces tilted up to see what the commotion was all about.

"Stop it!" Jerry screamed, grabbing wildly at the window ledge behind him. "Put me down!"

Jerry had the edge of the window frame in a death grip.

"Hey, don't worry, Flack," Gabe said from inside the window. "We won't drop you on your head or anything. We just want the picture of you hanging out the window, screaming your head off."

Jerry was, in fact, screaming his head off.

"Let me in! Stop it, Gabe! Let me in!"

"Smile for the camera, Flack!" Craig called.

Dangling headfirst out the second-floor window, Jerry was scared to death. The ground was so very far below. He began to feel sick to his stomach.

He was so terrified and sick, he wasn't aware he had started to cry.

"Please, Gabe!" Jerry sobbed. *"Let me in!"*

"What?" Gabe called out. "I don't think the people on the ground can hear you. Scream louder."

"Let me in!" Jerry screamed.

"Oh, okay," Gabe said. He and Craig dragged him inside. Jerry collapsed on the floor, gasping, trying to get control of himself.

The door of the classroom burst open, and Mr. Trent, the eighth-grade science teacher, rushed in.

"What's going on here!" he thundered.

"Nothing," Gabe said innocently. "Flack's okay. Aren't you, Flack?"

Jerry still couldn't get control of his breathing. He heaved in breaths of air with huge, gulping sounds.

"Jerry? Aren't you Jerry Flack?" Mr. Trent asked. "Are you all right? What happened here?"

Jerry felt Mr. Trent's hand on his shoulder.

He shook his head. He wasn't sure he could speak. "Nothing," he said, finally, in a rush of air. "I'm okay."

"What happened?" Mr. Trent asked for the third time.

"I—uh—I was leaning out the window," Jerry said, rising unsteadily. He pointed with a shaking hand to the oak outside. "I thought there was a bird's nest. But I slipped and nearly fell."

Mr. Trent frowned skeptically. "That's what happened?" he asked.

"Yeah," Jerry said.

"These guys didn't force you out the window?"

"No," Jerry said. "Really. I just slipped."

"We pulled him inside," Craig said, smiling. "Sure was a good thing we came along when we did. Old Jer here was screaming his head off. Right, Gabe?"

"Right." Gabe looked serious. "He was one scared dude."

Jerry didn't think Mr. Trent believed a word of their story. But he wouldn't tell on Gabe and Craig. He'd done enough screaming and crying while hanging out the window to strip his ego to the bone. He didn't need to cry to the teacher about what these bullies had done to him.

How many kids had been down below, watching his terror and humiliation? It had looked like about thirty or forty. If Cinnamon and Robin took pictures, they'd be passed around school Monday, and everyone would be pointing at him once again.

Mr. Trent told the boys to go home, and he waited, his arms folded, while they trailed out of his classroom.

"See you Monday, Flack," Gabe said when they were out in the hall. "I'll bring the best pictures. I'm sure lots of people will want to see them."

Jerry didn't respond. He set his jaw and stalked away. He just wanted to go home. To be by himself and nurse his wounds.

Jerry hated himself at that moment. Hated his cowardice, his terror of heights, his screaming while he was hanging out the window.

He wished that he could run away from Spencer Lake and never return.

How could he ever come back to school? How could he face the kids who saw him hanging out that window? And everyone who would see the pictures Monday?

Then he realized that some of the kids who were standing below might not have gone home yet.

Jerry went into the bathroom and ducked into the farthest stall. He waited for ten minutes, twenty, then thirty. He couldn't face the students who might be outside the building.

Finally, after forty minutes, he walked out of the bathroom, down to the main floor, then back to the custodians' room. The place was empty, so he hurried out the door, onto the loading dock, and across the athletic field.

He'd have to circle back to get home. But maybe everyone would have gone by then. He hoped so.

Jerry felt horrible about himself. He knew what he was. And by Monday, everyone at school who hadn't known before would learn the awful truth about him.

He was a lily-livered, weak-kneed coward. And still very much a dork.

And what's more, he thought, he was a dork on the run.

Chapter Thirteen

Jerry wasn't going to tell his mother what happened, and he didn't feel like pretending nothing was wrong. So when he got home, he retreated to his room.

He flopped back on his bed and squeezed his eyes shut, but all he could see was the view he'd had, hanging upside down, outside the science-room window. He felt a spasm in his stomach.

He thought of the students below, their faces turned up to see where the screaming was coming from. He thought about the pictures Cinnamon was taking, and he writhed in shame. He hated that he'd been so scared, he'd screamed bloody murder in front of all those kids who'd watched from below.

He wished again that he could run away so he'd never have to face any of them ever again.

For a long time, Jerry lay on his bed marinating in his own anger, frustration, and embarrassment. He knew he was wallowing in self-pity, and he hated himself for doing it. But he didn't know how he could possibly live through this—how he could handle this whole thing with even a modicum of cool. He'd already shown everyone what a terrible coward he was. Cowards are definitely not cool.

Finally, after a half hour, Jerry was sick of turning it over in his mind. He got up, sat at his computer, went to the web, and idly typed "self-defense" in the search box.

Jerry knew he wasn't the type to take up tae kwon do or judo in a serious way. Besides, a skill like that required years of training. But, Jerry thought, it would be quite satisfying to imagine himself using some good moves that could put Gabe Marshall on the floor.

He wished he could have used something on Gabe that would have prevented him and Craig from shoving him out that window.

A listing of various types of martial arts flashed on the monitor. He ran down the list and stopped at aikido. He'd never heard of it. *"In aikido, there is no punching or kicking. One uses an opponent's own energy to deflect an attack and throw him into a fall."*

What a concept.

Jerry read on. A weaker person who is skilled in aikido, the article said, can throw a heavier, stronger person around the mat simply by using the graceful, flowing movements he has learned. He uses his opponent's own strength and energy to subdue him.

Jerry sighed. If only he had started studying aikido when he was three years old, maybe he'd be good enough to deflect Gabe's attacks now.

Jerry sat back in his chair and stared out the window. He wished the devastation in his life could be fixed. But it was impossible. Once you've made a complete and utter fool of yourself, there's no turning back.

Why, Jerry thought, did I ever agree to run for sixth-grade president? He wished his family could move again, and he could start all over in a new town. He'd learned some powerful lessons about what *not* to do, and maybe he could find a way to fit in somewhere else.

But what about Brenda? a small voice asked in his head. She was a true friend, the best friend he'd ever had. He didn't want to lose her. He wondered what she would say when she heard about what had happened to him. Then he had a horrifying thought: what if she'd *seen* him hanging out the window and was too embarrassed for him to come and see how he was?

But he knew better than that. Brenda had stuck

by him before; she would continue to do so.

Hysterical barking outside drew his attention to the window. It sounded like Sassy in the front yard. Jerry ran to his parents' bedroom and looked out the window. Sassy danced near the curb in the front yard, growling and yapping at a large dalmatian across the street.

The dalmatian appeared to be debating with himself about whether to answer Sassy's challenge to leave her turf alone. He apparently decided to call her bluff and headed straight for her.

"Oh, no." Jerry ran out of the room and dashed down the stairs.

"What's wrong?" his mother asked from the living room.

"Sassy's in trouble." He jerked open the front door.

"If there's a dog fight, you stay clear," his mother said, hurrying up behind him.

But the trouble was over before it started. Sassy, her tail between her legs, rushed into the house between Jerry's feet. She whipped around, barking ferociously from the foyer rug.

Pretty brave inside the safety of her house, Jerry thought.

The dalmatian stopped in the middle of the front walk. He snorted with contempt, turned, and trotted away.

"Good dog," Jerry's mother said to Sassy. "You

stay away from big dogs that can hurt you."

The phone rang, and Jerry's mother disappeared into the kitchen to answer it.

Jerry patted Sassy's head. "You fit into this family just fine," he said softly. "Somebody picks on us, we cave in, hide, or run away. What's the matter with us, girl? Last I checked, we all had backbones."

"Jerry?" his mother called from the kitchen. "Phone's for you."

"Who is it?" he asked.

"I don't know."

Jerry climbed the stairs to his parents' room and picked up the receiver.

"Hello?"

"Hi, Jerry. It's Cinnamon."

"Oh. Hi." Jerry wondered if Cinnamon would start giggling about what Gabe had done to him.

"First," Cinnamon said, "I want you to know that when Gabe told me to take pictures of you up in the window at school, I didn't know what he was going to do."

"You mean, you didn't take the pictures?" Jerry asked, his heart suddenly bursting with hope.

"No, I took a whole roll."

"A whole roll?"

"Well, that's what Gabe told me to do. I wouldn't have done it otherwise."

You don't think for yourself? Jerry wanted to say. But he didn't. He waited to hear why she had called.

"Monday I'm going to tell Gabe that I'm quitting his campaign," Cinnamon said.

Jerry was surprised. "Why?" Did she think so little of Gabe after his mean tricks that she was going to resign from his campaign in protest? That would make a powerful statement.

"Why? Because he keeps flirting with Zoey and trying to get her attention," Cinnamon said. "And I'm supposed to be like his girlfriend."

"Oh." That was all.

"I might even campaign on your side," she said.

To get even with Gabe, Jerry thought.

Still, having Cinnamon on his side would give him one more vote. He'd still lose, but by one less vote for Gabe.

"Okay," he said.

"Well, I thought you should know," she said. "See you Monday."

"Oh, Cinnamon?" he said quickly before she hung up. "You were on the ground below the window, right?"

"Yeah."

"Well, how—I mean, what were the other kids like? I mean, when they saw me up at the window?" Did they laugh? he wanted to ask her. But he didn't.

"Well, at first," Cinnamon said, "everyone thought you were being murdered or something."

"Murdered?"

"Because of all the screaming."

"Oh." Jerry felt his face heat up. He wished he hadn't asked.

"But then they realized that Gabe and Craig were holding you out the window. I guess they were just curious, watching to see if you'd accidentally fall headfirst from the second floor."

"Oh." Jerry said again. This was awful. "Just a minute." He covered the mouthpiece with his hand. "Okay!" he called out. "Cinnamon?" he said into the receiver. "I have to go eat supper. See you later."

"See you."

Jerry hung up and collapsed on the rug next to his parents' bed. Sassy trotted in the room and licked his face. A whole roll of film, he thought miserably, scratching the dog's neck. He wondered if the camera had a zoom lens that captured the terror on his face as he hung out the window. The pictures would be passed all over school Monday, and the kids would want to see that look on his face. Especially after they heard about how he'd screamed.

Even the nice kids would want to see the pictures. It would be sort of like the perverse curiosity that draws people to the scene of an accident. They'd want to see Jerry's torment, even if they thought Gabe was a jerk for pulling the practical joke on him.

And they'd probably not vote for Jerry for president. Who would want a geek like him running the sixth grade?

Jerry dragged himself back to his room. He'd stay there till supper, so he wouldn't have to answer any probing questions from his mother about how his day went.

Jerry managed to get through supper without either of his parents suspecting anything was wrong. It had been hard to sit at the table and push food into his mouth when he didn't feel like eating. It was difficult to concentrate on the chitchat and participate in ordinary dinner table conversation when a hard lump had formed in his chest. It throbbed with an ache he'd never experienced before. He had never felt so miserable.

"Jerry, will you tell Melissa to clear the table?" his mother asked after supper. "She bolted before I remembered it was her turn."

"Okay."

Jerry hadn't even noticed that Melissa was gone. He wasn't thinking about anything but getting back to his room. Maybe he'd even go to bed early tonight, so he could escape from thinking about what had happened at school.

He went to the family room. Melissa sat cross-legged on the couch and stared at the TV screen, her eyes glazed over.

"Hey, Melissa," he said. "It's your turn to clear."

Melissa didn't respond or turn away from the TV.

"Melissa?" Still no response. *"Melissa?"*

Now she looked up and frowned. "What." It was a demand, not a question.

"Your turn to clear."

She blew out an exasperated breath. "I hate clearing."

Jerry's mind took him back to the dinner table. He was so miserable himself, he hadn't realized until now that Melissa had been very quiet during the meal, too.

Jerry said, "Melissa, you want to play a game of Battleship later?"

"No," she said emphatically. She got up and stomped into the kitchen.

Jerry watched her go. Melissa had changed a lot since she'd met Cory. Jerry figured the third grader was still pushing Melissa around. Why did Melissa want to play with Cory when Cory was so mean to her? Did she think Cory was cool? Was it just because Cory was older? It didn't make sense to Jerry.

He shrugged. He had his own problems to worry about. He got up and shuffled upstairs to spend the rest of the evening in his room.

"What about performing a science trick?" Brenda suggested. "That could be impressive."

It was Saturday afternoon. Jerry and Brenda sat

cross-legged on the floor of his room, brainstorming ideas for Jerry's campaign speech. Sassy lay with her head resting in Brenda's lap.

"Yeah, maybe," Jerry said.

He was having trouble concentrating. He hadn't told Brenda yet about what had happened at school yesterday. He couldn't bring himself to talk about it. It was all too fresh in his mind, too painful. What if he got tears of embarrassment in his eyes? He couldn't risk it.

"You want to look through your science magazines for something that might work with a speech?" Brenda asked.

"Oh, okay," Jerry said, staring at the floor. "I guess."

"Jerry?"

"Yeah?"

"You're awfully distracted," Brenda said. "Are you okay?"

"Yeah." He continued to avoid looking in Brenda's eyes.

"I heard about what Gabe did to you yesterday after school."

Jerry's head snapped up. "You did? Who told you?"

"Kim and Kat were waiting for their bus under the eighth-grade science window."

Jerry closed his eyes. "It was pretty embarrassing," he said.

That was, of course, the understatement of the year.

Brenda's voice was soft. "You want to talk about it?"

Now he opened his eyes and gazed directly at her. "Maybe I should drop out of the race."

"And give Gabe the satisfaction of knowing that his cruel tricks worked?" Brenda asked. "Do you want Gabe Marshall to be head of the sixth grade?"

"No," Jerry said. "But Brenda, I don't know if I can take any more of this. You don't know what it feels like to be a laughingstock."

"You're *not* a laughingstock," Brenda said.

"If I'm not now, I will be Monday, when all the pictures of me hanging out the window are passed around at school."

"Oh, I hate Gabe for what he's done to your self-confidence," Brenda said.

"Bren, there's no way I can win the election. That's why I'm thinking about quitting. That, and I can't stand any more humiliation. Besides, it would be embarrassing if Gabe wins in a landslide. There's no way I can win."

"That's not true, Jerry Flack," Brenda said. "And after you win, I'm going to take you out for dinner to celebrate."

"Thanks for the offer, Bren," Jerry said. "But you know as well as I do, that's a very safe bet."

"Just you wait and see, Flack," Brenda said. "I have confidence in you."

I do, too, Jerry thought. Confidence that Friday, voting day, will be the most embarrassing day of all.

Chapter Fourteen

Jerry took a deep breath as he neared the school Monday morning. He figured that, right away, someone would make a comment about Friday's window incident. Last night, he'd practiced in the mirror what to say if anyone teased him. He planned to shrug it off and pretend it wasn't a big deal. "Oh, it was scary at the time, but I've completely forgotten about it!" was a line he liked a lot. He'd also practiced laughing in a believable way and saying, "Remind me never to go into politics."

Jerry hoped he'd remember to use these lines when the time came. He also hoped his face wouldn't get red and give him away. He mentally braced himself as he entered the school.

Cinnamon was waiting for Jerry at his locker. She looked upset.

"Can I talk to you, Jerry?" she asked.

"Uh, sure." Was she going to show him one of the pictures she'd taken of him hanging out the window? Had Gabe given her one already?

"Not here," she said. "Maybe in the media center, where it's quiet?"

"Okay."

Jerry followed her down the hall and into the media center. Only a few students were there, working on computers and looking for books.

Cinnamon led him to a study carrel. She pulled out the chair. "Sit here." She dragged another chair over and planted it next to him.

This must be something awful, Jerry thought, to bring him to a place this isolated. Did she think he was going to cry or something? His pulse quickened.

Cinnamon planted herself in the second chair and gazed at Jerry, her eyes troubled.

"Just tell me," Jerry said anxiously. "What is it?"

"I need advice," Cinnamon said.

Jerry blinked. "Advice?"

"Yeah. I thought you might be able to help me. See, I want to hang out with Zoey so bad."

This was about *Zoey*? Jerry let out a breath. He could already feel his body start to relax.

"See, I didn't go out for cheerleading because I knew Zoey would think that was dumb. But it didn't help. She still won't talk to me, unless I ask her a question or something."

Cinnamon sighed heavily. "How should I talk to her? She's so cool, every time I'm around her, I feel like a—" She glanced around to see if anyone might be listening and whispered, "Like a dork."

Jerry felt his mouth pop open. He closed it. *"You?"* he asked. "You feel like a—"

"Shhh!" Cinnamon slapped a hand over his mouth. "I don't want this to get around." She looked over her shoulder and turned back to Jerry. "Yes. I admit it. I feel kind of dorky around her."

"Amazing." Jerry considered what Cinnamon was saying, and a revelation presented itself to him. "Do you think—I mean, hypothetically speaking," he said, the excitement building inside him, "Do you think it's possible that dorkiness is on a kind of sliding scale? Depending on who you are, there's nearly always someone cooler who can make you feel like a dork? That's really fascinating."

Cinnamon rolled her eyes. "Whatever. I just need you to help me with this."

"Why me?"

"Because, let's face it, Jerry, you've had a lot of experience with this problem—no offense—and you're so *brave* about it. I mean, here you are at school, after Gabe made you look so stupid last week! If I'd been humiliated like you were, I'd be at home, crying my eyes out."

"Oh." *Thanks* wasn't the right word here.

But, Jerry thought, Cinnamon was right about one thing. He was the perfect person to give advice about dorkdom.

"Well," he said, "I know how you feel. And I've done some reading on the subject, on how to rise above those feelings of inadequacy. For instance, 'Dear Abby' and various teen magazines say that a good way to create a friendly environment is to ask the other person about things he or she is interested in."

Cinnamon frowned.

"So what interests Zoey?" Jerry asked.

"Nothing," Cinnamon said. "Everything bores her."

"Is there anything that makes her laugh?" Jerry asked. "Or gets her enthusiastic or excited?"

"Nope."

"Nothing?" Jerry asked.

"Nothing. And come to think of it, I've never seen Zoey smile."

"Really?" Jerry asked. "Have you ever considered that maybe the problem is in Zoey and not you?"

Cinnamon's eyes widened. "But *she* doesn't have a problem. She's the coolest person I've ever met!"

"Let me ask you something," Jerry said. "Why would you want to hang out with a girl who has no interests and never gets excited about anything? She sounds pretty dull to me."

"Zoey? Dull?" Cinnamon gazed at Jerry in disbelief. "You've got to be kidding. Everybody wants to be *like* her! Haven't you seen the kids imitating her?"

"Yeah," Jerry said. "But it doesn't make any sense to me."

Cinnamon sighed. "I guess you can't help me, Jerry. You just don't understand."

"Sorry," Jerry said. He leaned forward. "But Cinnamon, you can't change who you are. If she doesn't like you for yourself, you can do without her."

"Do without her?" Cinnamon cried. "Easy for you to say!" And she added sarcastically, "Thanks a lot."

She got up and stalked out of the media center.

Jerry stared after her. Sometimes, he thought, it seemed as if the people in his class were from a planet in a solar system that was millions of light-years away.

No wonder he was having trouble with the campaign.

It was just before language arts class that Jerry saw the pictures of him hanging out the school window.

"Over here," Brenda said outside the language arts classroom. She led him to the far wall. "I wanted you to see them before Gabe waves them in front of your face," she added in a low voice. "I guess he had dozens of copies made. They're already getting passed around in the halls. I grabbed as many as I could."

She held up the first one.

"Oh, geez," Jerry said, wincing. He slapped a hand to his forehead. "She used a telephoto lens."

"Sorry," Brenda whispered. "This is the worst one."

It was a close-up, all right. The whites of Jerry eyes were showing around the irises, and his mouth was wide open in a scream, frozen in time, frozen in terror.

Jerry flipped through the rest of the pictures. They were all bad, all humiliating shots of him screaming and struggling while Gabe and Craig held him upside down out the window.

"Oh, man. What are people saying?" he asked in a whisper.

Brenda paused. "About what you'd expect."

"They're laughing?"

"Some. Others are angry at Gabe and Craig. Depends on who you talk to."

"But everyone's looking at the pictures," Jerry said.

"Yeah," Brenda agreed. "They're all looking." She glanced back over her shoulder, and Jerry followed her gaze. A group of four seventh graders was pointing at him and laughing.

"See what I mean?" Jerry whispered. "By the end of the day, everyone in school will have seen the pictures. And they'll all be laughing."

"You know," Brenda said, "you could get Gabe and Craig into deep trouble with these pictures. They should be expelled for doing something so dangerous. What if you'd fallen from the window?"

"I'd be dead," Jerry said. "But getting them in trouble wouldn't make things better. The pictures would still be there."

"But Gabe can't run for sixth-grade president if he's expelled."

"Brenda, I don't want to win the election by default."

"I know," Brenda said, sighing. She put a hand on his arm. "It was just a thought."

Ms. Robertson smiled from the classroom doorway and waved at them to come in.

"Come on," Jerry said, stuffing the pictures in his pocket. "Time for class."

"At least we know Gabe won't say anything during language arts," Brenda said.

"Why not?"

"He can't flaunt the pictures in front of a teacher. He must know he'll get in big trouble if any adult at school sees the evidence."

"Right," Jerry said. "I hadn't thought of that."

At least he was safe through language arts class, he thought. But when he walked into the classroom,

Gabe and all his friends at the back of the room stifled laughs.

All except Cinnamon. She had changed her place and was now sitting back by the windows, next to Zoey. She and Zoey were slumped in their seats, looking bored out of their minds.

"So what do you think will happen next?" Kim asked Jerry at lunch. "This campaign has been pretty exciting. A new, entertaining episode every day."

"It's got to be over," Jerry moaned. "It has to be."

"Maybe if you stayed home till the speeches on Friday, you'd be safe," Tony suggested.

Jerry thought about all the kids who had nudged friends and snickered as he passed in the hall this morning. "You don't know how tempting that is," he said. "You think I should wave a white flag in front of Gabe's face? 'I give up! You win the dirty tricks war. I'm not playing anymore'?"

"You stick to the high road," Brenda said. "If Gabe pulls anything else, it'll be such overkill, it'll explode in his face. Everyone will hate him."

"Unless it's funny," Kim offered. "Everyone likes a funny practical joke." She caught Brenda's ferocious glare and slunk down in her seat.

"Hey, Jerry!" a girl called out, walking past with a group of three friends, holding their lunch trays. "We saw your picture. What a riot!" They laughed.

"No, seriously, Gabe was mean to do it, but the picture was really funny." They laughed again and moved away.

"See?" Jerry said. "Gabe has a ready audience, just waiting for whatever he'll do next."

Jerry just hoped if Gabe was going to pull anything else, it would be something little. At least, something that couldn't kill him.

Chapter Fifteen

Jerry was heading for PE, when Zoey stepped out of a classroom doorway. She lifted her head, which for Zoey, was a major attempt at communication.

"Hey, Zoey," Jerry said, curious. "What's up?"

"A word of warning," she said in a low voice. "Gabe told me he has another surprise for you in PE today."

Jerry caught his breath. "*Already?* Did he hint at what it might be?"

"I don't think Gabe is capable of hinting. As you've probably noticed, subtlety isn't his strong suit," Zoey said. "He didn't come right out and tell me what it was. So be on guard."

"Thanks," Jerry said. Zoey nodded and started to turn. "Zoey? How come you told me?"

Zoey's expression didn't change. "Because Gabe's an idiot. And you've taken enough abuse from him."

"Well, thanks."

Zoey disappeared back into the classroom.

Jerry took a couple deep breaths. He continued walking toward the gym at a slower pace, trying to prepare himself. What would it be this time?

Ever since Gabe had stolen his clothes from his locker basket, Jerry had used a new lock and stood very close to it while he worked the combination so no one could see. What else, besides stealing Jerry's clothes, could Gabe to do him? He wasn't even in Jerry's PE class.

Jerry changed into his gym clothes and locked his clothes in the basket.

Today, everyone—both boys and girls—was jogging and walking around the quarter-mile track outside. One lap was to be jogged, the next walked. Then they were to come inside to play dodgeball. The sky was purple and threatening to rain any minute.

Mr. Gunther led everyone in stretches for their hamstrings and quadriceps.

"Okay, let's get going," Mr. Gunther called out when the stretching was finished.

Jerry kept looking from side to side, waiting for something awful to happen. He walked the first lap to warm up, then began to jog. He caught up with Nick Fenneman and jogged alongside him.

"Saw the picture of you hanging out the window," Nick said. He didn't smirk, so Jerry figured he wasn't on Gabe's side.

"Yeah," Jerry said. "I heard Gabe was going to do something to me this hour, but so far, so good."

"Oh, really?" Nick suddenly looked uncomfortable, and Jerry realized that Nick was probably hoping he wouldn't get hit with whatever was planned for Jerry. "Well, guess I'll push it a little. See you."

"Oh, sure."

Nick put on some speed and moved out ahead of Jerry.

Safely away from me, Jerry thought. He decided he should've kept his mouth shut.

Jerry was beginning to heat up. Inside his shorts, an uncomfortable sensation bothered him. At first, it itched. But moments later, it began to burn.

What's that? Jerry thought. The burn was in a very bad, personal place. He couldn't scratch, or someone might notice.

The burn intensified, and all at once Jerry knew what Gabe had done. He'd put something on his athletic supporter! Something that would set him on fire when he heated up in PE.

Jerry began to run toward the locker room.

"Hey, Flack! Where are you going?" Mr. Gunther called to him.

But Jerry couldn't stop to explain. He felt as if he were on fire. He had to get to the locker room and take off all his clothes and jump into a cool shower.

"Yikes, yikes, yikes," Jerry wailed as he ran.

A figure stepped out from behind the edge of the building.

"Smile, Flack!" Gabe called out from behind his camera.

Jerry heard the shutter click a half-dozen times before he reached the locker room door and rushed inside.

He threw off his clothes—which smelled suspiciously like Ben Gay—ran to the shower, and frantically turned the faucets till the water was gushing all over him.

After the fire was out, under the streaming water, Jerry realized that this might be the most embarrassing trick of all. Everyone—even the *girls*—would know why Jerry had made a mad dash to the locker room during PE class.

This was definitely a funny trick, just like Kim had said. At least it would be funny to everyone else. So it *wouldn't* backfire on Gabe. Everyone would be laughing and smirking at Jerry Flack, the butt of all the jokes. The dork who had dared to run against a popular guy for sixth-grade president.

Gabe could've smeared the Ben Gay on Jerry's athletic supporter very easily through the openings in the wire basket that held his gym clothes. Jerry wouldn't have been aware of the Ben Gay smell when he put on his clothes. The locker room, particularly near the end of the day, reeked with odors of sweat and antiperspirant.

Jerry couldn't stand it any more. He couldn't face Mr. Gunther. He couldn't face the other guys. And he sure couldn't face the girls after the story got around. Not even Brenda. Not this. It was too personal.

Jerry dressed in his street clothes, left the locker room, and walked into the hall. He pushed open the heavy door to the outside and trudged down the sidewalk toward home.

No one was around when Jerry arrived. He went straight to his room and stayed there.

The phone rang just after school was out, and Jerry ran down the hall to his parents' room to check Caller ID. The call was from a pay phone. Probably from school, probably from Brenda. It rang ten times, but he didn't pick it up.

Jerry decided maybe he should take Tony's advice and stay home the rest of the week. At least after the voting was over and Gabe had been elected president, he wouldn't have a reason for playing these horrible tricks on Jerry. Jerry could slink back to school, and after awhile, maybe people would forget.

He pictured himself *slinking* back the following Monday, and he cringed. What kind of a person has to sneak to school, hoping not to be noticed? Hoping not to be taunted, teased, tormented?

A scared, pathetic excuse for a boy, that's who. Jerry hated himself and hated what he'd become.

But he'd proven to himself that trying to get even with Gabe didn't work. Not only did it escalate Gabe's need to embarrass him, Jerry didn't like the way he felt about himself.

So if Jerry didn't want to be a bully, and he couldn't stand being the victim of humiliation, what could he do?

There wasn't an answer, he thought. It was either fight or run. If he stood still, Gabe would just hit him again with another embarrassing prank.

Jerry flopped back on his bed and closed his eyes. He had never felt this miserable.

Voices from the backyard rode the breeze through Jerry's open window. He could hear Melissa talking, and there was another voice. Was it Rachel?

Jerry opened his eyes and sat up. Good, he thought. It was Rachel, Melissa's friend from her first-grade class. Maybe Melissa had decided that Rachel was a better friend than Cory.

The two girls climbed into the tree house.

"Hey, Melissa!" Cory and her two third-grade

friends swung the gate open to the backyard.

"Hi, Cory," Melissa called back. But she didn't sound enthusiastic.

"We want to play in the tree house now," Cory said.

Melissa hesitated. "Well, okay," she said.

"So you and your little friend have to leave," Cory informed her.

Even from the window, Jerry could see Melissa's eyes widen. *"What?"* she said.

Cory was already climbing the ladder.

"Yeah. Me and my friends are gonna play alone," Cory said. "Remember, you said I could play here anytime I wanted to."

She stepped into the tree house, followed by her friends. Cory stood at least a head higher than Melissa and used that to her advantage, standing threateningly close to the smaller girl. "So you'll have to get out now. You and pip-squeak here." She jerked her thumb toward Rachel.

Jerry clenched his teeth. "Don't let her push you around, Missy," he whispered.

A new look came into Melissa's eyes. Jerry had seen it lately around home. It was a look of anger, of defiance, of strength.

"This is *my* tree house, Cory," Melissa said, her voice strong and scornful. "*You* get out! And your friends, too."

Cory glanced back at the other girls, then turned

again to Melissa. Her voice was softer but threatening. "We don't want to leave. If we do, I won't be your friend anymore."

Melissa scowled. "Good! Because you know what? I don't even *like* you anymore!"

"Yes!" Jerry said quietly. He nearly applauded but stopped himself. "Good for you, Missy," he whispered.

"Okay," Cory said. "But you're pretty selfish if you won't share the tree house. Didn't you ever learn about sharing?"

"Nope, I never learned about it," Melissa said, her faced tipped up, glaring at Cory.

A look of relief spread over Melissa's face as Cory and her friends climbed down from the tree house. After the three girls had left the yard, Melissa beamed at Rachel. "You know what, Rach? That felt real good!"

Rachel laughed. "You were awesome, Melissa."

Jerry grinned, then caught a glimpse of himself in the mirror over his bureau. His smile faded.

If only he could stand up to Gabe the way Melissa had stood up to Cory. But his situation was more complicated. Gabe wasn't just commandeering Jerry's tree house. He was playing horrible tricks to humiliate Jerry.

Jerry sank to his bed, wishing that life were as simple as it had been in first grade. Still, watching Melissa stand up to Cory just now gave Jerry strength. If Melissa could stand up to a bully, Jerry decided he could at least go back to school tomorrow and face his classmates.

It wouldn't be easy. No doubt, those smirking, sneering students would be passing around pictures of Jerry racing to the locker room to put out the fire in his shorts.

"Hey, Jerry," Brenda said on the phone that evening.

She called me 'Jerry,' Jerry thought. She knows about the Ben Gay thing.

"Hey, Brenda." Jerry tried to force a lightness into his voice, but it came out too loud and phony. "What's up?"

"Well, I wondered why you weren't in computer class today. Then I heard about the rotten thing Gabe did to you in PE. I'm really sorry."

"It was all over school before the last bell, I bet," Jerry said.

"Pretty much," Brenda said. "That would've been hard to keep a secret."

"Yeah."

"I don't know why Gabe won't stop," Brenda said. "Enough is enough."

"He won't stop because all the kids are wondering what he'll do next," Jerry said. "And this probably made the best gossip of all."

"I guess you're right," Brenda said. "You're coming back to school tomorrow, aren't you?"

"Yeah." Jerry sighed. "I suppose I'll be in trouble for skipping the last two periods."

"You know," Brenda said, "if you'd tell what happened, you won't get in trouble. Gabe will."

"I'm not going to rat on Gabe," Jerry said. "Then I really *would* be a wimp."

"I figured you'd say that," Brenda said. "So I told your last two teachers that you weren't feeling well and went home. I told the attendance secretary the same thing."

"Oh, thanks, Bren," Jerry said.

"No problem." She paused. "They said you should've stopped in the nurse's office. But I don't think you'll be in much trouble. You have a strategy for handling tomorrow?"

Jerry nervously fingered the curly telephone cord. "Uh, I guess I'll try and laugh it off."

"That's probably the best idea," Brenda said.

Jerry sighed. "Know what, Bren? I'll be so happy when this election is over. I just want to get back to normal. If that's possible."

"Sure, it's possible," Brenda said. "Don't worry, Flack. By next week at this time, it'll all be behind you. You'll think of it and laugh."

"Sure," Jerry said. He didn't think that was likely, but he noticed that Brenda was calling him Flack again. Maybe that was a sign that things would be back to normal before too long.

It couldn't happen soon enough.

Chapter Sixteen

"If the election is decided by advertising, you'll win big," Brenda said, gazing around at the school walls the next morning.

She had met Jerry at his locker, and they were headed toward language arts class. "Gabe didn't put up more than two or three posters," she said. "And look." She pointed to a poster that was drawn with a black marker on white paper. Vote for Gabe Marshall for Sixth-Grade President, it said. "Pretty uninspired. He must've made it, himself."

"His posters might be dull," Jerry said. "But he sure puts a lot of imagination into his dirty tricks."

"Yes, indeedy. He certainly does."

Two girls walked past, watching Jerry, giggling

and whispering behind their hands. Halfway down the hall, it happened again with three eighth-grade girls, and a minute later, with a couple of sixth-grade boys.

Jerry focused his gaze on the floor ahead of him, so he wouldn't have to see any more of the smirks that were following him down the hall.

"Hey, Flack!" Jerry looked up and saw a boy standing at his locker. Jerry didn't know him but thought he might be an eighth grader. "Was it hot enough for you yesterday?" The kid laughed. "Man, Gabe Marshall's making a geeky sucker out of you!"

"Glad you're so easily entertained," Jerry blurted. The kid's grin faded; he shut his locker and stalked away. Jerry turned to Brenda. "I shouldn't have said that."

"I think you should answer these jerks," Brenda said, scowling. "Don't just lie down and take it."

"Gabe has already won," Jerry muttered. "No matter what happens with the election, he's won because—that guy was right—Gabe's made a geeky sucker out of me."

"Don't you talk like that, Flack," Brenda said. "Don't even think it."

As he neared the language arts classroom, Jerry slowed. He didn't want to go into the room and see Gabe. Everyone would be watching and waiting to see what would happen between them.

"This'll be the worst part," Brenda whispered.

"After you get through this, the rest of the day will be easy."

Jerry nodded, took a deep breath, and walked into the classroom.

Gabe was already there, sitting with his usual fans, except Cinnamon, who had changed her seat to sit near Zoey.

"Hey, look who's here; it's Hot Pants," Gabe said. He picked up an envelope and waved it. "I got some great shots of you running to the locker room. You should see your face." He laughed, and the girls sitting around him snickered.

Ms. Robertson walked into the classroom.

"Stick around after class, Flack," Gabe said. "I'll show you the best pictures." He added in a whisper, meant to be heard all over the classroom, "Flack is so photogenic."

More laughter.

Jerry dreaded the end of class, when he would probably have to face Gabe again. The period dragged. Jerry had a hard time concentrating on Ms. Robertson's lesson on the elements of mystery novels. He had his own villain to deal with.

After language arts was over, Jerry got up and walked out of the classroom.

"Hey, Hot Pants. Wait up."

Jerry felt his cheeks blaze as Gabe caught up with him. The rest of the students, apparently hoping for a good show, hurried out after Gabe. They all gathered around the two boys. Jerry was grateful for Brenda's hand on his arm.

"Don't you want to see the pictures?" Gabe asked, pretending surprise. He pushed a handful of photos into Jerry's hand. Jerry stuffed them into his pocket without looking at them.

A voice behind them said, "Gabe, stop being such a jerk."

Jerry turned to see Cinnamon standing on his other side.

Gabe gaped at Cinnamon as if he couldn't believe his ears. "What?" he said.

"Jerry, do you have any extra campaign buttons?" Cinnamon asked.

"Uh, yeah," Jerry said.

"Great." Cinnamon took the button that Jerry dug out of his book bag, and she pinned it on her shirt. She gave Gabe a look of triumph. "I left your campaign last week, but you didn't even notice," she said. "You're too busy thinking about other things—and people."

Now Gabe's face was turning red. "So what? See if I care. Go ahead and wear the dork's campaign pin."

He turned to Jerry and gave him a hard shove. Jerry stumbled back and landed on his butt on the floor.

"Come on, Flack," Gabe said, beckoning him to

get up. "Don't be such a wimp."

Jerry was aware that more kids were joining the crowd to watch Gabe torment him. His face continued to blaze hot, and his stomach was full of butterflies. He felt like a fly that was about to have his wings pulled off by some rotten kid who just wanted to watch him writhe in agony.

But then, as Jerry sat on the floor, feeling humiliated and angry, a miracle happened. The miracle was in the form of a Wonderful Idea, and it suddenly sprang into Jerry's mind, fully formed.

"I'll meet you," Jerry said. "After school."

"Yeah, right."

Jerry got up and brushed himself off. He looked around. Seventh and eighth graders had joined the crowd. "No, really," he said to Gabe, suddenly feeling much better. "I'll meet you after school. We'll get this settled once and for all."

Gabe showed Jerry a sly smile. "I'll meet you in the commons," he said. "We'll go from there."

"I'll be there," Jerry said. He tried a smile, and it felt genuine. "Right after school."

Gabe stared at Jerry suspiciously, then apparently decided he couldn't lose any kind of showdown with Jerry, and his sneer returned.

"Great," he said. "This'll be so fun."

Gabe, followed by his entourage, turned and strode down to the water fountain.

"Jerry?" Jerry turned to see Ms. Robertson gazing

at him through the crowd. "May I talk to you for a moment?"

"Sure," Jerry said. He nodded to Brenda and shouldered his way through the crowd, following Ms. Robertson back into the classroom. The rest of the students who had watched the confrontation between Jerry and Gabe began to move on their way.

"Jerry, I've been concerned about you lately," Ms. Robertson said slowly, as if she were measuring her words.

Jerry felt his body tense, but managed a casual, "Oh, why?"

"Well, I've been hearing stories about nasty jokes played on you," she said. "I didn't see what happened out there just now, but Gabe was clearly bullying—bothering you."

"Oh, that." Jerry forced a laugh and waved his hand. "Gabe was just—he likes practical jokes. He's just being Gabe. He's quite a character."

Ms. Robertson seemed to search Jerry's face for clues about the truth. "I'd be very concerned if I learned that any student was being harassed. There's no room for that kind of behavior at school."

Jerry nodded. "Thanks. I appreciate it."

"So you're okay?" she asked, frowning.

"Yeah, I'm okay." Jerry smiled. "But thanks for asking."

She smiled, but Jerry had the feeling she didn't really believe him. "So how's the campaign going? I saw your website. It looks great."

"Thanks." Jerry was glad that Ms. Robertson hadn't seen the pictures he'd posted last week of Gabe the Monster. "The campaign's going okay."

"Well, good," she said. "I guess you'd better take a break now before everyone is back here for social studies."

"Right."

Jerry smiled again and loped into the hall where Brenda was waiting.

"Everything okay?" Brenda asked.

"Sure," Jerry said. "She'd heard rumors about Gabe's tricks. I told her not to worry about it."

"So you're really going to meet Gabe after school?" Brenda asked, her brows a couple of caterpillars, inching together.

"Yeah," Jerry said. "I got this great idea. Want to help?"

"Sure." Brenda looked surprised. "What do you have in mind?"

"Something like a showdown."

Brenda's eyes widened. "With Gabe? You have a death wish or something?"

Jerry grinned. "Meet me in Mr. Hooten's room at lunchtime."

"I'll be there."

Jerry's legs trembled as he and Brenda walked toward the commons area after school.

"So you really gonna fight Gabe?" a kid hollered at him across the hall.

"Nope," Jerry said. "I just said I'd meet him, and we'd settle it."

"Haw!" the boy exclaimed. "We'll see what Gabe says about that! Everybody's gonna be there."

Jerry nodded at him.

"I sure hope this works," Brenda said.

"Jerry. Jerry." Kim and Kat Henley appeared alongside him.

"Hey," he greeted them.

"What's going to happen?" Kim asked.

"I don't know," Jerry said. "I hope nothing much."

"This feels like high noon in some old Western movie," Kat said. "You know, the two guys about to draw their guns on each other."

"Yeah," Kat said, "it's really exciting because you know that one of them will be dead by the end of the scene."

"Kat," Brenda warned.

"Okay, okay."

They rounded the corner, and Jerry caught his breath.

A crowd of about a hundred students waited in the commons area.

"Geez." It came out of Jerry in a whisper. Brenda squeezed his arm.

Gabe, already waiting for Jerry, sat propped

against a small table. He looked up and smirked when Jerry approached.

"So we gonna fight, Flack?"

"How about a test of strength?" Jerry asked him.

Gabe sputtered out a laugh. "You and me? You gotta be kidding!"

Jerry shrugged and glanced around the commons. A large soda machine stood against one wall. Empty cans stood in crates on the floor, waiting for recycling.

"How about this?" Jerry walked to the nearest crate and picked up a soda can. "Can you tear this in half?"

Jerry tossed the can to Gabe, who caught it and scowled. "Of course not, Hot Pants. Nobody can tear a soda can in half."

He threw it at Jerry, who tried to catch it, but it clunked against his head and fell on the floor. Some of the kids laughed.

Jerry leaned down and picked up the can. He casually wrapped his hands around it and ripped it in half.

A gasp rushed through the crowd. "Did you see that? He tore that can right in two! *Cool!*"

Jerry smiled. He strolled back to the crate, picked up another can and tossed it to Gabe, who caught it in one hand. "Want to try?"

Gabe's eyes narrowed. "It's some kind of trick. You can't rip a can in half. You're a wimp."

"Try it," Jerry said. "Try and rip it."

Gabe glowered at Jerry and fired it back. This time, to Jerry's amazement, he caught it. He was so surprised, he laughed. Then he tore the can in half.

Everyone whooped and applauded. Jerry looked around and saw a couple of teachers at the edge of the crowd, watching. They looked as impressed as the students did.

Gabe's face was getting redder by the minute. He stormed to the crate, pulled out a can and tried to rip it.

Nothing happened, and everyone laughed.

"I *told* you it was a trick, Flack!" Gabe hollered. "You can't rip a can in half."

"You got that right, Gabe." Jerry grinned. "It *is* a trick."

"How'd you do it? Tell us," the kids called out. "That's so cool."

"It's pretty simple," Jerry said. "At lunch, I took those two cans out of the crate and used a blade from Mr. Hooten's room to scratch a line around the inside of the cans. Then I made a solution of 9.9 grams of copper chloride and 100 milliliters of water and poured it into the cans."

"That did it?" asked Tony. "It weakened the can?"

"Yeah," Jerry said. "I rolled the solution around inside the cans where I'd scored them with the blade. Then I put the two prepared cans back into the crate and remembered where I put them, so I could pick them out when the time came." He grinned at Gabe who glared back at him.

"That's so cool," someone called. "Can we try it?"

Jerry shrugged. "Sure. Maybe we could have a demonstration of science tricks after school sometime. That'd be fun."

Gabe stormed off, but the students didn't seem to notice. They began to leave, still murmuring about the cool can trick. Mr. Hooten, watching from nearby, flashed a grin at Jerry and left.

Zoey stepped forward from the milling crowd of kids. She didn't speak or smile, but she gave Jerry a thumbs-up. He nodded, and she disappeared into the mob of kids moving toward the school's exit.

Brenda clapped a hand on Jerry's shoulder. "Well, Flack, I have to say that was impressive," she said. "How'd you know that Gabe wouldn't try to rip the two cans in half?"

"Oh, that wasn't too hard," Jerry said. "Gabe knew he couldn't tear a can in half, and he didn't want to look dumb, so I figured he wouldn't try the first time. And he thought I wouldn't give him a chance to rip a can that I'd 'fixed,' so he passed up the second one, too."

"What a suspicious boy he is," Brenda said, grinning. "You know something, Flack? You're brilliant to have figured out how he'd react."

"It was a lucky guess."

"And modest, too!"

Jerry laughed. "Come on, Brenda. Let's go home."

Jerry was as surprised as he was elated that his plan had worked. He hadn't felt this good since he'd started his campaign. He threw an arm around Brenda's shoulder, and they headed for the door.

Chapter Seventeen

Jerry was still feeling great about the soda-can trick that evening. He sat at his desk, working on math homework, but his mind kept replaying the scene in the commons. He'd loved the looks on the kids' faces when he'd ripped that first can in half. Their mouths hung open, and their eyes nearly popped from their heads.

Jerry remembered what he'd read about the martial arts known as aikido. In aikido, you can deflect your opponent's attack by redirecting his energy so that he falls away from you.

That's something like what Jerry had done with Gabe. Gabe had wanted some kind of showdown—a fight, a show of strength. So Jerry gave him a showdown, but not using physical strength. Instead, he put his own spin on the confrontation. He had redirected Gabe's energy and guided him into a gentle fall. Jerry hadn't been hurt. And except for Gabe's bruised ego, he hadn't been hurt, either.

It had been a victorious day. Jerry gave a satisfied sigh and went back to his math problems.

The doorbell rang a few minutes after Jerry's family had finished dinner.

"I'll get it," Jerry's dad said.

Jerry wasn't expecting anyone, so he headed up the stairs.

"Jerry?" he heard his dad say. "Yes, he's here. Come in."

Mr. Flack turned to Jerry. "A girl named Zoey's here to see you. She says she'll wait outside." He left the heavy door ajar and went into the living room.

Zoey's here? Jerry descended the stairs and pushed open the screen door.

Zoey stood a few yards away, off the stoop. Her hands were stuffed into the pockets of her jeans, and she stared down the street.

"Hey, Zoey," Jerry said.

Zoey's face held the same blank expression as usual. "Have some news for you."

"What?"

"Gabe's next plan."

"Again? Already?" Jerry felt his chest deflating.

"Why does he tell you this stuff?"

Zoey shrugged. "Let's face it. He's an idiot."

"But you've made it clear that you're not on his side."

"He likes to brag. He thinks maybe he'll impress me. Go figure."

Jerry mentally braced himself. "Okay," he said with an exasperated sigh. "What's he going to do *this* time?"

"You know those pictures he's been taking of you? Crawling over the ice, hanging and screaming out the window, running for the locker room—?"

"Yeah, yeah." Jerry didn't need reminding. He knew every one by heart.

"Gabe's going to use those in a special poster campaign. They'll be plastered all over the school tomorrow, the pictures with slogans like, Do you want this DORK for president of the sixth grade? and Jerry Flack is a dork! You know, stuff like that."

"And the voting's in just a few days," Jerry moaned.

"Thought you'd want to know Gabe's plan," Zoey said.

"Yeah," Jerry answered. "I guess it's better to hear it now than be surprised at school tomorrow when all the posters go up."

But Jerry's heart was sick. He didn't have the stamina for this. Just when things looked better, Gabe was going to remind everyone of all the humiliations Jerry had suffered in the last ten days. Gabe would pick at Jerry's scabs till they were all freshly bleeding again. And the kids were laughing.

Jerry collapsed on the stoop and put his head in his hands. "I give up," he said. "I can't fight him. I knock him down, and he just gets up and comes after me again and again."

Deep in his misery, he was aware that Zoey had sat down next to him.

"Flack, I think you were superb today."

Jerry turned to gaze at her. "Really?" He was amazed to hear something so positive coming out of Zoey's mouth.

"Yeah," Zoey said. "Do some more of that."

"What? Science tricks?" Jerry asked.

"Whatever. See you, Flack." Zoey got up and shuffled down the front walk. Jerry watched her and noticed that she wasn't slumping as much as usual. That was weird. Zoey sure was a puzzle.

Jerry was amazed that she had taken the trouble to come to his house to warn him about Gabe's plan. Maybe he had misjudged her. Maybe she did care about something after all.

Fair play. Maybe that was it.

"Thanks," he called after her. She continued walking and didn't acknowledge that she'd heard.

"Brenda? Hi, this is Jerry."

Jerry sat on the bed in his parents' room and

curled the telephone wire nervously around his finger. The humiliating photos that Gabe and Cinnamon had taken were piled on the floor.

"Hey, Jerry!" Brenda said. "Are you still glowing from your triumph this afternoon? It was great that so many kids were there."

"Well, Zoey just told me about Gabe's next plan."

"Already? You're kidding!"

"Nope. Gabe's going to plaster the walls at school with those pictures of me he took in—well, those embarrassing situations." Jerry hugged the phone against his ear with his shoulder and spread the pictures out on the floor. He gazed around at them and winced. "The posters will ask the kids if they really want a dork for president."

A long silence followed. "Gabe's such a dirty player," she said finally. "He realized his stupid platform wasn't effective, so he decided to attack you."

"You have to admit, it got him a lot of attention," Jerry said. "And me. I just keep thinking, Bren, everyone will remember me as this dorky kid who dared to run against a cool, popular guy."

"Gabe isn't cool," Brenda said. "But this last trick will get people's attention, all right. And remind them as they walk down the halls."

"I wish I could just—. Wait." An idea was suddenly forming in Jerry's head.

"What?"

"I wonder—?" He touched a few of the photos on the floor.

"Tell me what you're thinking," Brenda pressed.

"I wonder if I could use Gabe's weapons to foil him?"

"What do you mean?"

"Bren, can you come over for a while? I think I have an idea."

"You bet. What are we going to do?"

"Try a little mental aikido with Gabe."

"A little what?"

"Come over, and I'll explain," Jerry said.

"Be right there," Brenda said and hung up.

Brenda laughed as they walked into the school building the next morning with a mob of students. "Gabe's plan is going to blow up in his face," she said. "I can't wait to see what he says when he sees *our* posters." She patted a bunch of them under her arm.

"We'll see," Jerry said. "It depends on what the kids think of our work. Come on. Let's hang these on the walls before Gabe can get his posters up."

They hurried to the main corridor on the ground floor.

"Here," Brenda said, handing him a poster from the top of her pile. "This is a good one."

Attached to their poster was one of Cinnamon's photographs of Jerry hanging out the science-room window, his mouth frozen open in a terrified scream. The caption read, Hang Out with the Dork! Vote for the Dork for President!

Two girls Jerry didn't know stopped to read the poster.

"Wow," one of them said. At first she looked surprised to see the picture on Jerry's poster. Then she read the caption and laughed. "Oh! That's funny."

"Good going, Jerry," the other girl said. They smiled as they walked on.

"The first two people liked it," Brenda said. "That's a good sign."

"Here," Jerry said, walking farther down the hall. "Let's put one by the entrance to the cafeteria."

Brenda pulled out another poster. This had the picture of Jerry sprawled on the ice. The caption read, Spread the News! Dorks are COOL! Vote for Jerry-the-Dork Flack!

A crowd of sixth graders nearby read it and laughed.

Upstairs, near Ms. Robertson's classroom, they put up a poster with a picture of Jerry running—on fire from Ben Gay—toward the locker room. Who's Hot? the caption read. Jerry-the-Dork Flack will run far to get your vote! Vote for the Dork!

Nick, from his PE class, called out, "Now *that's* funny, Flack!" He gave Jerry a high five.

"What'd I tell you?" Brenda whispered. "Flack, you're brilliant. You're beating Gabe at his own game."

"It's like aikido," Jerry said. "I can't fight him. So I'm just using Gabe's own energy—and idea—to deflect his attack."

"Well, whatever it is, it's working."

They hung a dozen posters upstairs, a half dozen near the gym, then decided to hang the rest near the front door. As they put up their last poster, Brenda glanced over Jerry's shoulder and whispered, "Here comes Gabe."

Gabe had the confident stroll of a guy who was planning to win an election. He carried a bunch of posters under this arm. He saw Jerry and hollered, "Hey, Flack! You're the star of my new posters."

"What a coincidence," Brenda said. "Jerry's the star of *our* new posters, too."

Gabe stopped in front of the Ben Gay picture, and he became quiet while he read. His expression went from self-assured to mystified.

He snorted. "You're calling yourself a dork?"

"Yup," Jerry said casually. "I can't fight it, Gabe. Might as well own up to it."

A group of students walked past and read Jerry's poster and laughed. A girl from the crowd called out, "Flack, has anyone ever told you what a good sport you are?"

"Thanks," Jerry said.

"So, Gabe," Brenda said, turning to him. "Let's see your posters."

Gabe glanced down at the posters he was carrying.

"I uh, I—have to get to my locker before first period." He hurried away down the hall.

Brenda laughed and put out her hand. "Flack, has anyone ever told you what a good sport you are?"

"Just a second ago, but tell me again." Jerry didn't shake her hand, but held on to it.

"Everyone loves a good sport, and this proves it," Brenda said. "You're going to win this election yet."

"Think so?" Jerry said. "I'm not so sure."

"What do you mean?"

"The look on Gabe's face," Jerry said. "I defeated him, and every time I've been able to do that, he comes back attacking harder than ever."

"True," Brenda said. "But you're learning how to handle him. Aikido, remember?"

"Yeah," Jerry said. "I just hope I can always figure out how to do it."

"Only a couple of days left."

"Yeah," Jerry said. "I wonder what he'll do before Friday?"

"Probably something," Brenda said.

"Most likely," Jerry said. He sighed. "I'll just have to be ready."

Chapter Eighteen

For the next two days, Jerry nervously walked the halls at school, waiting for Gabe's next strike. After school, he and Brenda worked on his speech, and he practiced it in front of the mirror to make sure his delivery was okay.

All the while, part of Jerry's mind was hunched over in readiness, like a runner taking his mark before the race. Ready to spring into action to deal with whatever Gabe dished out.

But Gabe was quiet in class and didn't try anything underhanded. Which made Jerry more nervous than ever.

Friday morning, the day of the voting, Jerry dressed in his favorite distressed jeans and his cool, faded T-shirt. The hair gel made his hair obey perfectly and lie flat, just as he wanted it to. But he was so on edge, he couldn't think about anything but his speech—and what Gabe might pull at the last minute.

"I wish Gabe would just do whatever he's going to do," Jerry said to Brenda before school. "The waiting is almost as bad as having to deal with the humiliations."

Brenda shrugged. "Maybe there aren't going to be any more humiliations," she said. "Maybe Gabe realizes he can't beat you in this election."

It was true, Jerry thought, the students had responded overwhelmingly in favor of Jerry's Vote for Jerry-the-Dork campaign. But he truly doubted that Gabe would give up without a last-minute trick to make Jerry look stupid on voting day.

"You've practiced your speech, and you're ready to go," Brenda said.

"I'm nervous."

"You'll be great," Brenda said with conviction.

Jerry wished he shared her confidence.

The morning wore on. Jerry had a hard time concentrating in class. He kept checking the clocks. He was anxious to give his speech and get it over with.

Slowly, the hands of the clock inched their way to 1:15. It was finally time to get ready for the 1:30 assembly. Jerry ducked into the boys' bathroom. The place was empty.

He slipped a comb out of his pocket and turned toward the mirror.

The bathroom door whispered open, and Gabe and Craig sauntered in.

Jerry gazed at them warily. "Hey," he said.

Something was up. He felt the hair on his arms and the back of his neck rising in alarm. He couldn't help notice that the two boys were blocking his only way out of the bathroom.

"What's up?" he asked, trying to sound casual.

"Let's do it," Gabe said.

"What?" Jerry asked.

The boys rushed at him and wrestled him to the floor.

"Wha—what are you doing?" Jerry cried, struggling under their weight.

"I got him," Gabe said. He was sitting on Jerry's chest, with Jerry's arms pinned under his knees. Jerry could hardly breathe. "Do it," Gabe ordered.

Craig sat on the floor at the top of Jerry's head, so Jerry couldn't see him. But he felt him. And he had no doubt what Craig was doing.

Snip, snip, SNAP.

Craig was cutting off chunks of Jerry's hair.

"No!" Jerry yelled. "Stop it!"

He struggled as hard as he could, but Gabe's grip on him only tightened.

"Hurry up!" Gabe demanded.

"I'm cuttin' as fast as I can," Craig said.

173

Snip, snip, snip. Snip, snip, snap.

"Stop!" Jerry hollered. "Stop that!"

"Okay, that's good," Gabe said.

The scissors were silent, and the boys released Jerry.

"Let's get outta here," Gabe said.

Gabe and Craig ran out of the bathroom, leaving Jerry gasping on the floor, with handfuls of hair piled around his ears.

He sat up and felt his hair. "Oh, no," he whispered. He struggled to his feet and gazed at himself in the mirror. *"Oh, no!"* he moaned.

Huge sections of his hair were gone, leaving numerous nearly bald patches all over his head.

"Oh, geez," he wailed. "Oh, *geez.*"

A boy from his computer class walked in. "Whoa," the boy said, stopping dead in his tracks. "What happened?"

"I—I ran into a wild pair of scissors," Jerry said.

How could he go out in the hall looking like this? How could he deliver a speech to the sixth grade looking like this? The assembly was due to start— he checked his watch—in seven minutes.

The boy seemed to have forgotten why he'd come into the bathroom. He stood frozen, staring at Jerry.

Brenda should be arriving at the gym for the assembly any minute. He'd have to go find her. He took a deep breath and rushed out into the hall.

The sixth graders were all heading to the gym for the assembly. At first, they stared, then they poked one another, and stared some more, and started talking.

"D'you see Flack? Parts of his hair are gone!"

"Look, he's over there!"

"Oh, gross, man!"

Jerry kept walking fast till he spotted Brenda. She and the Henley sisters were heading for the gym.

"Brenda!" he called.

She turned to see him and let out a strangled cry. "What happened?" she whispered. "Did Gabe do this to you?"

"Find somebody with a cap," he said. "I'll be just inside the bathroom door at the end of the hall."

"Good idea!" She ran off down the hall, while Kim and Kat stared at him.

"Oh, wow," Kat whispered.

Jerry turned and hurried back to the bathroom, while students continued to point at him and comment on how "gross" and "demolished" and "totally wrecked" he looked.

In less than a minute, Brenda tapped at the door, and Jerry opened it. "Here," she said, shoving the cap at Jerry.

"Thanks." He slipped the cap on his head. "Come on, the assembly's about to start."

Jerry forced himself—surrounded by staring, laughing students—to walk to the gym. The story about his hair had spread like a wildfire in a wind-storm. "Hey, Flack! Let's see your hair!" one boy called out to Jerry. Jerry didn't know him, but he'd seen him hanging out with Gabe a few times. Jerry ignored him.

"I think you're supposed to sit with the candidates over here." Brenda pointed to some chairs lined up near the far wall.

Jerry nodded and walked to the edge of the room. Gabe was already seated. An empty chair sat next to him. Gabe smirked. "Have a seat," he said.

Jerry walked past him and sat in a chair that was three down from Gabe.

Jerry felt for the notes in his pocket. They were still there. He took a big breath and looked around.

Most of the students had arrived and filled the bleacher seats in the gym. All the candidates for the sixth-grade elections were present and seated in the row where Jerry sat.

Ms. Robertson walked to the podium, which stood in the center of the floor in front of the bleachers, and called the assembly to order.

"This is your last big chance," she told the sixth graders, "to learn what your candidates stand for. Listen carefully and consider what they say. At the end of the assembly, we'll pass out ballots. You will vote and drop your ballots in either of the two boxes near the doors on your way out.

"Now, may I first introduce the candidates for

sixth-grade class treasurer," she went on.

Each of the candidates got up and gave a short speech about why they wanted to be treasurer. The speeches were okay, Jerry thought, but they both tilted toward boring. The students in the stands shuffled their feet and murmured a lot between speeches.

The vice-presidential speeches weren't any more interesting. But Jerry would have had a hard time concentrating on them, anyway. He was still reeling from Gabe's and Craig's attack in the boys' bathroom. Adrenaline was pumping through his veins, and he was breathing so fast, he was afraid he'd hyperventilate and faint. He forced himself to slow his breathing and relax his muscles.

It was a good thing Brenda had found a cap for him to wear. He couldn't possibly sit here, in front of the entire sixth grade, with chunks of his hair gone.

Then it was time for the presidential candidates to give their speeches. An uncommon hush came over the students sitting in the stands. They were ready to hear what these two boys, who had battled it out in the halls, had to say about running for president.

Gabe's turn was first. He strolled to the podium and aimed his charming smile at the crowd.

"Who do you want to run the sixth grade?" Gabe asked. "Someone who is cool or"—he paused and glanced over at Jerry—"someone who's a dork?" Laughter ran through the audience. "It's not that Jerry Flack isn't smart, because he is. But what kind of image do we want to head the sixth-grade class? Are we a class of smart, dorky geeks? We've seen, during the last two weeks, that Flack isn't athletic, he's scared of heights,"—this got some laughter—"and he isn't cool. And really, do we want a guy with these skinny, white legs to run our class?" Gabe held up an enlarged photo of Jerry walking the halls in his gym shorts.

The crowd laughed louder.

"If you think the late rule needs to die, I'll work on that, too. And we'll get video games in the detention room. Thank you."

The students applauded, and about a dozen friends of Gabe's, scattered throughout the bleachers, thrust their fists in the air shouting, "Gabe, Gabe, Gabe, Gabe!"

Gabe didn't leave the podium until he saw Jerry get up and walk toward it. Gabe strolled back toward his seat, but as he was passing Jerry, his hand snapped out, and he grabbed the bill of Jerry's cap. But Jerry had expected it and hung on. Gabe laughed and let go. He loped to his seat while the sixth graders talked and laughed in response.

Jerry pulled the notes out of his pocket and tipped the microphone down to his level. He looked out over the crowd.

"Take off the cap!" someone shouted from the back.

"Yeah, Flack!" a boy in front called out. "Take off the cap. We want to see your hair."

A handful of boys began chanting, "Take off the cap! Take off the cap!"

Jerry looked at the boys who were chanting. All of them were Gabe's friends and, no doubt, had been instructed by Gabe to disrupt Jerry's speech.

More kids picked up the chant, and, soon, nearly half the class was calling for him to take off his cap.

"I'm Jerry Flack, and I'm running for sixth-grade president," he said, starting out on his prepared speech.

But the kids didn't stop chanting. "Take off the cap! Take off the cap!" they shouted at him.

Jerry looked over to see Ms. Robertson get up from her chair and start walking across the gym floor in his direction. He couldn't let her demand that the kids be quiet. He'd really look like a dork then.

Aikido, he thought. Don't fight it. Use it.

Jerry pulled off his cap, and the kids suddenly hushed, staring at his ravaged hair with an odd mix of humor and horror on their faces.

"A funny thing happened on the way to the gym," Jerry said. "Let me tell you, it was a hair-razing experience."

Some of the kids in the bleachers groaned. Some laughed and hooted, and others applauded.

By this time, Ms. Robertson stood next to him.

Jerry covered the microphone with his hand. "It's okay, Ms. R. Everything's cool."

Worry lines etched her face, and her gaze skimmed over his wrecked hair. She whispered, "I want to talk to you after the assembly."

He nodded to her and turned back to the kids while Ms. Robertson returned to her place by the gym entrance.

Jerry looked out over the bleachers and made up his mind. He folded his notes and tucked them back into his pocket.

"I was going to talk about how we need someone to make exciting things happen around here," Jerry said. "But, as you probably know, things have been pretty exciting—for me, at least—during these last two weeks."

Some kids laughed and applauded.

"Instead," Jerry said, "I want to talk to you about dorks." He waited a moment while the gym got completely quiet. "Because, as Gabe has pointed out, I am one." Jerry spread out his arms. "That's right; I'm a dork. Dorks tend to run in my family." He counted off on his fingers. "I'm scared of heights, I'm not athletic, I don't look like a movie star, and I have skinny, white legs.

"But, see, I don't mind being a dork. All my

heroes are dorks—every one of them. Albert Einstein, Stephen Hawking, Bill Gates. Those are the famous ones. But we all know dorks. Some of them sit next to you in class. Some of the grown-up dorks take care of you when you're sick; they discover new medicines; they run Wall Street and the biggest corporations in the country; they send human beings into space. I bet whoever comes up with a cancer cure will be something of a dork." He shrugged. "Maybe it'll be me. Maybe it'll be someone else in this class."

Jerry knuckled his glasses back up on his nose.

"I think dorks are pretty cool. So if you think you have any dork tendencies, don't hide them, afraid that people will put you down. You're in good company. Stand up and say, 'I'm a dork, and I'm honored to be part of such an esteemed group of human beings.'"

That got some laughs.

Jerry paused, then said, "I'm done with my speech, but I'd appreciate your vote for sixth-grade president. Thank you."

The sixth graders clapped. Some whistled; some hooted their support. Jerry grinned to the crowd and realized happily that most of the students were smiling back at him.

The announcement came over the intercom at the end of the school day. Jerry Flack had been elected president of the sixth grade.

Brenda, sitting next to Jerry in computer class, gave him a high five.

"You did it!" she said. "I knew you'd do it!"

"Thanks, Bren," he said. He was happy; he not only had lived through the two-week ordeal, he had won.

All the harassment, the humiliation, the worry—it was finally over. A heavy weight that Jerry had hauled around on his back for two weeks suddenly took wing and disappeared. He felt lighter than he had in a long time.

The bell rang, ending class, and they walked out into the hall.

The Henley sisters hurried over, along with Tony and Chad. "Congratulations, Jerry!" the girls called in unison.

"Did Ms. R. talk to you after the assembly about Gabe's attacking you?" Chad asked.

"Yeah," Jerry said. "I said it was okay, but Ms. R. said Gabe and Craig would probably be put on probation for a little while."

"I wish they'd kick 'em out of school," Kat said. "Gabe, especially. He deserves it for making you suffer so much."

"Oh, Gabe just likes keeping things stirred up," Jerry said.

Zoey appeared from a crowd of kids, with Cinnamon trailing along behind.